Abracadabra Cello

The way to learn through
songs and tunes

Maja Passchier

A & C Black · London

First published 1989 by A & C Black (Publishers) Ltd,
35 Bedford Row, London WC1R 4JH

Reprinted 1991, 1993, 1995, 1999

ISBN 0 7136 5637 9

Printed in Great Britain by Martins the Printers, Berwick upon Tweed

Music setting by Linda Lancaster

Cover by Alex Ayliffe and illustrations by Bernard Cheese

The publishers would like to thank Paul McCreesh, Lucy Wilson and Richard Wright for their help in the preparation of this book.

Contents

1 Clown dance

traditional French

Play these bars four times while your teacher plays the tune.
Play with the bow:

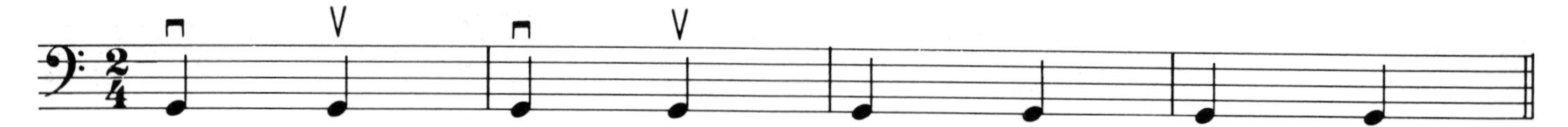

Teacher:

2 Bobby Shafto

traditional

You play:

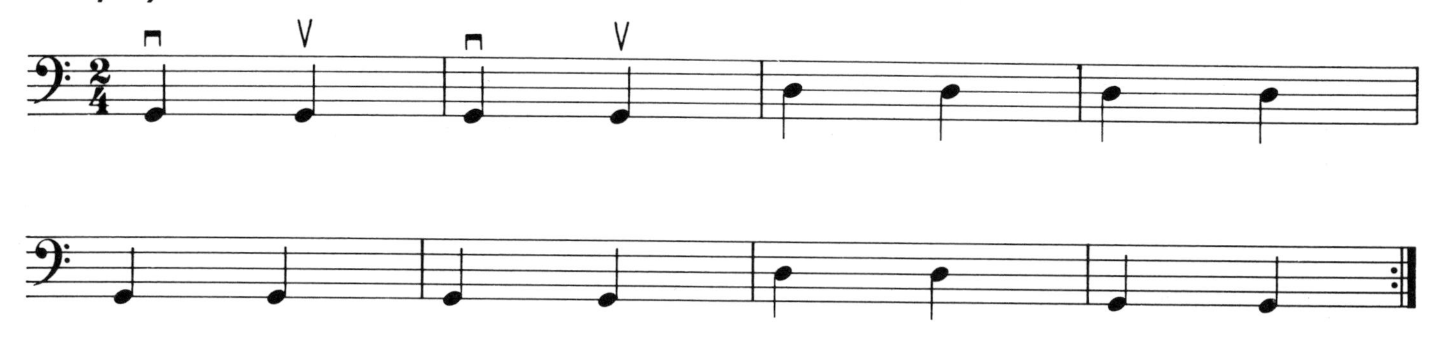

Teacher:

Bob - by Shaf - to's gone to sea,— Sil - ver buc - kles at his knee,—
He'll come back and mar - ry me,— Bon - nie Bob - by Shaf - to.

Bob - by Shaf - to's bright and fair, Comb-ing down his yel - low hair;
He's my own for e - ver more, Bon - nie Bob - by Shaf - to.

3 Au clair de la lune

traditional French

↗ *Lift the bow from the string so as to be ready to play a second bow stroke in the same direction.*

You play:

f (loud)
p (soft)
p
f
Teacher:

Play the next tunes (4 to 11) ***pizzicato*** *– that is, pluck the string with the right hand index finger. Then go back and play them with the bow.*

4 Frère Jacques

traditional French

Play these notes on the G string while your teacher plays the tune:

0 1 3 0 0 1 3

Teacher:

5 Suo-gân

Welsh

0 1 3 1 0 0 1 3
Win - ter creeps, Na - ture sleeps, Birds are gone, Flowers are none.

6 Hot cross buns

traditional

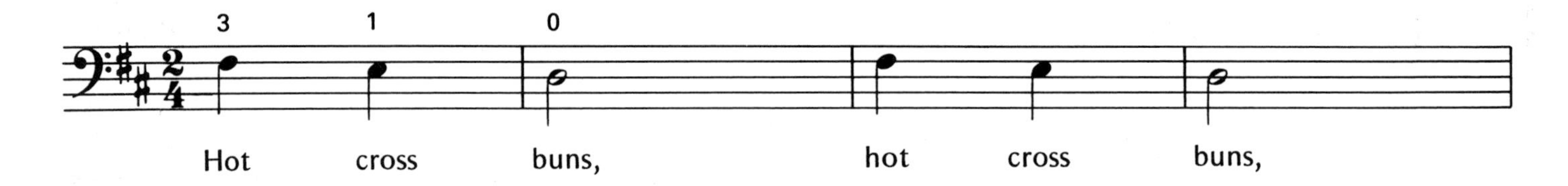

3 1 0
Hot cross buns, hot cross buns,

One a pen - ny, two a pen - ny, hot cross buns.

7 Now the day is over

S Baring-Gould

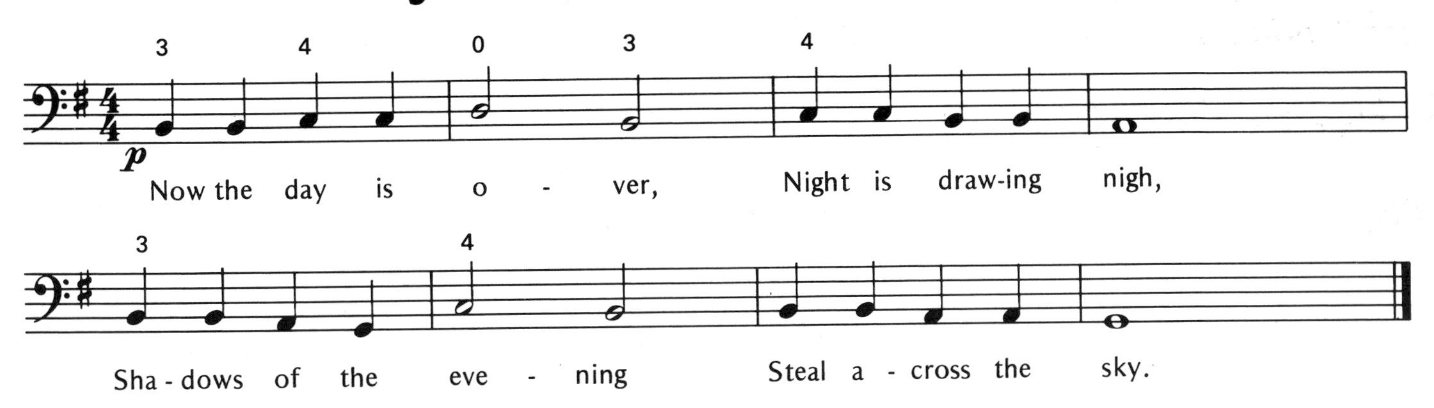
3 4 0 3 4
p
Now the day is o - ver, Night is draw-ing nigh,
3 4
Sha - dows of the eve - ning Steal a - cross the sky.

8 Old MacDonald's farm

traditional

4 4 4 0 1 1 0 1 4
Old Mac - Do - nald had a farm, E - I - E - I - O!
On that farm he had a cow, E - I - E - I - O! With a
moo, moo, here, and a moo, moo there, Here a moo, there a moo, ev-'ry-where a moo, moo.
Old Mac - Do - nald had a farm, E - I - E - I - O.

9 Au clair de la lune

traditional French

4 0 1 4 1
mf
p
p
mf

10 Little bird

German

11 Twinkle, twinkle little star

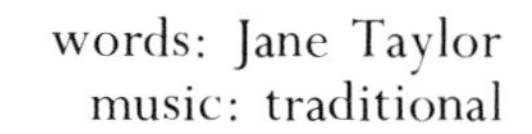
words: Jane Taylor
music: traditional

Twin - kle, twin - kle lit - tle star. How I won - der what you are.
Up a - bove the world so high, like a dia - mond in the sky.
Twin - kle, twin - kle lit - tle star. How I won - der what you are.

Now go back and play tunes 4 to 11 with the bow.

 *Slur – two or more notes played with the same bow stroke.*

12 Clown dance

traditional French

13 Love somebody

Folk song

14 Andrew mine, Jasper mine

words: C K Offer
music: Moravian carol

3
mf
Love some - bo - dy, yes I do, Love some - bo - dy, yes I do,
Love some - bo - dy, yes I do,
p
Love some-bo-dy but I won't tell who!
0 3 4 1
An - drew mine, Jas - per mine, Ti - mo - thy and A - bel,
Hur - ry to Beth - le - hem, to the com - mon sta - ble.
There you'll find a ba - by small, sleep - ing in a swad - dling shawl;
On your way, on your way, To our Sav - iour born to - day.

15 Buttercup

North American

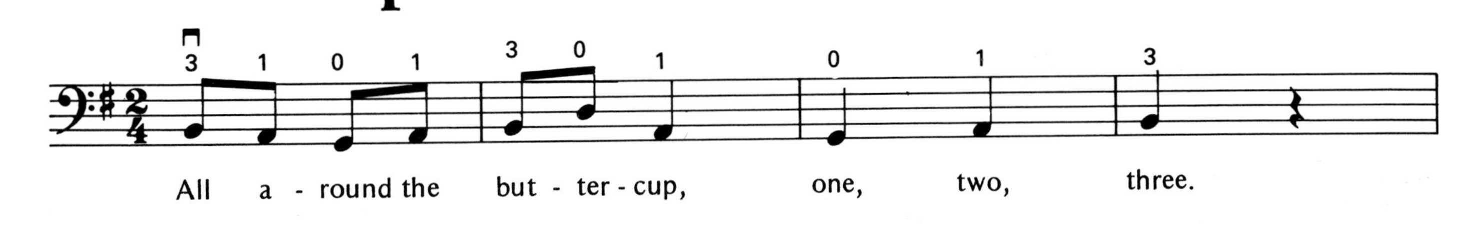

3 1 0 1 3 0 1 0 1 3
All a - round the but - ter - cup, one, two, three.

If you want a pret - ty maid, just choose me.

16 Frère Jacques

traditional French

3
Fre - re Jac - ques, Fre - re Jac - ques, *Dor-mez vous? Dor - mez vous?
*Son-nez les ma-ti - nes! Son-nez les ma-ti - nes! *Ding, dang, dong! Ding, dang, dong!
*entry point when played as a round
LIFTING THE BOW
17 Chatter with the angels
spiritual
Chat-ter with the an - gels, soon in the morn - ing,
Chat-ter with the an - gels in that land. Chat-ter with the an - gels,
soon in the morn - ing, Chat-ter with the an - gels, join that band.

18 Big Ben

traditional

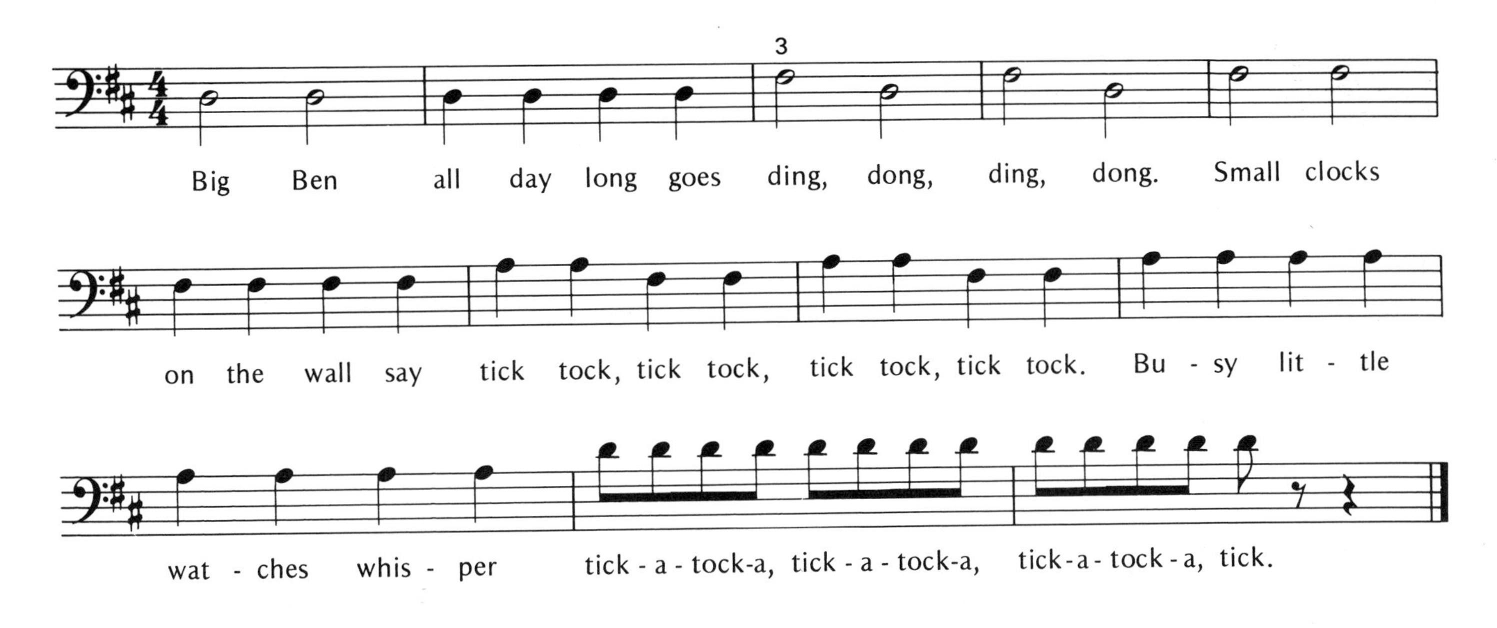
3
Big Ben all day long goes ding, dong, ding, dong. Small clocks
on the wall say tick tock, tick tock, tick tock, tick tock. Bu - sy lit - tle
wat - ches whis - per tick - a - tock-a, tick - a - tock-a, tick-a-tock-a, tick.

19 Baa, baa, black sheep

traditional

2 4
Baa, baa, black sheep, have you a - ny wool?
2
Yes, sir, yes, sir, three bags full. One for the ma - ster and
one for the dame, And one for the lit - tle boy who lives down the lane.

20 Shepherds' hey

Morris tune

2 4
f (second time p)
2
p (second time f)

21 Canon

Bartók (from Mikrokosmos)

Allegro moderato

22 Okki-tokki-unga

traditional

DC al Fine (sometimes just DC) – go back to the beginning and play to end at Fine.

Ok - ki - tok - ki - un - ga, Ok - ki - tok - ki - un - ga,
Hey, Mis - sa Day, Mis - sa Doh, Mis - sa Day. Ok - ki - tok - ki -
- un - ga, Ok - ki - tok - ki - un - ga, Hey, Mis - sa
Day, Mis - sa Doh, Mis - sa Day.
Fine
Hex - a col - a mish - a

won - i, Hex - a col - a mish - a won -
DC al Fine
i, Hex - a col - a mish - a won - i.

23 London Bridge

traditional

3
Lon - don Bridge is fall - ing down, fall - ing down, fall - ing down.
Lon - don Bridge is fall - ing down, My fair la - dy.

24 While shepherds watched

words: Nahum Tate
music: traditional

2
3
While shep - herds watched their flocks by night All seat - ed on the
2
ground, The an - gel of the Lord came down And glo - ry shone a - round.

25 Theme from the ninth symphony

Beethoven

3
4
mp
cresc.
dim.

26 Clown dance

traditional French

27 Lullaby of the spinning wheel

words: trans Taylor Coleridge
music: F T Durrant

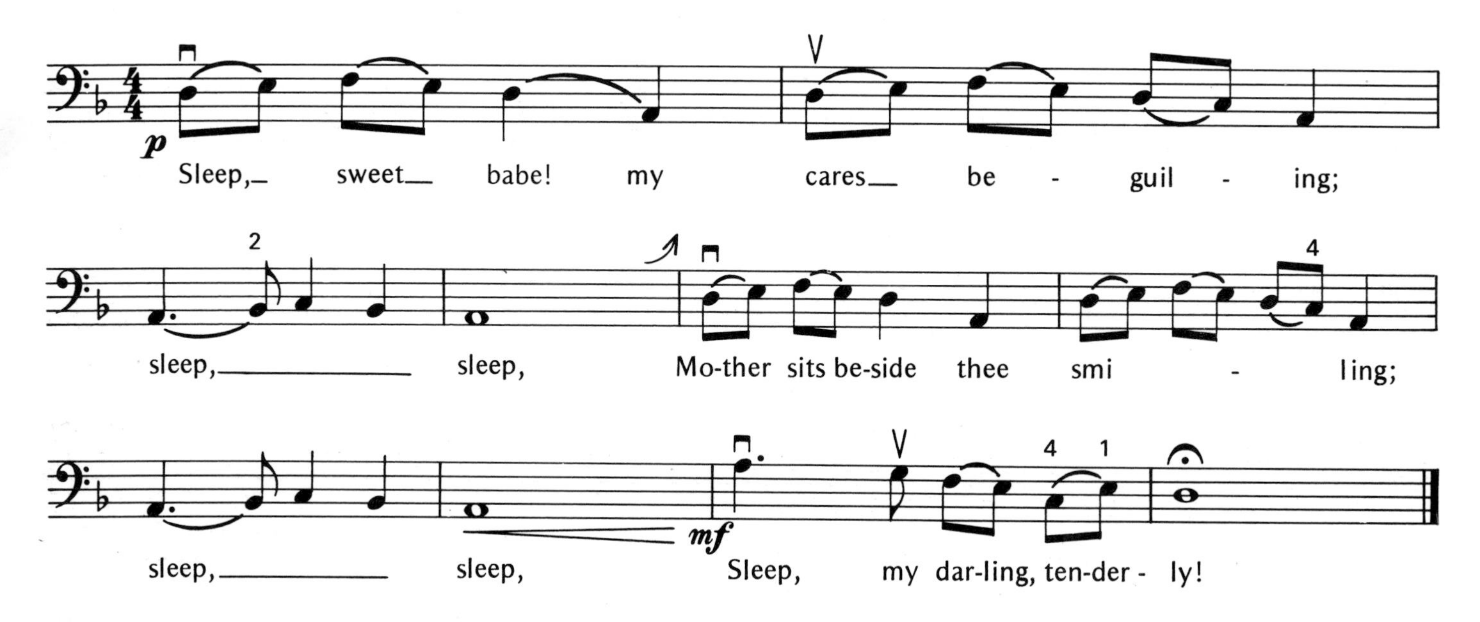
p
Sleep,— sweet— babe! my cares— be - guil - ing;
sleep,—— sleep, Mo-ther sits be-side thee smi - ling;
sleep,—— sleep, Sleep, my dar-ling, ten-der - ly!
mf

point = stay at the point end of the bow.

28 Michael, row the boat ashore

traditional

point
Mi - chael, row the boat a - shore, Hal - le - lu -
- yah! Mi - chael, row the boat a - shore, Hal - le - lu - - yah!

29 Last night I had the strangest dream

Ed McCurdy

Last night I had the stran - gest dream I e - ver
dreamed be - fore. I dreamed the world had
Fine
all a - greed to put an end to war. I
dreamed I saw a might - y room, the room was
filled with men. The pa - per they were
point
DC al Fine
sign - ing said they'd ne-ver fight a - gain.

30 London's burning

traditional

Lon-don's burn - ing, Lon-don's burn - ing * Fetch the en - gines, Fetch the
en - gines, *Fire! Fire! Fire! Fire! * Pour on wa - ter, Pour on wa - ter!

*entry point when played as a round

31 When the saints go marching in

traditional

W.B. = use the whole bow.

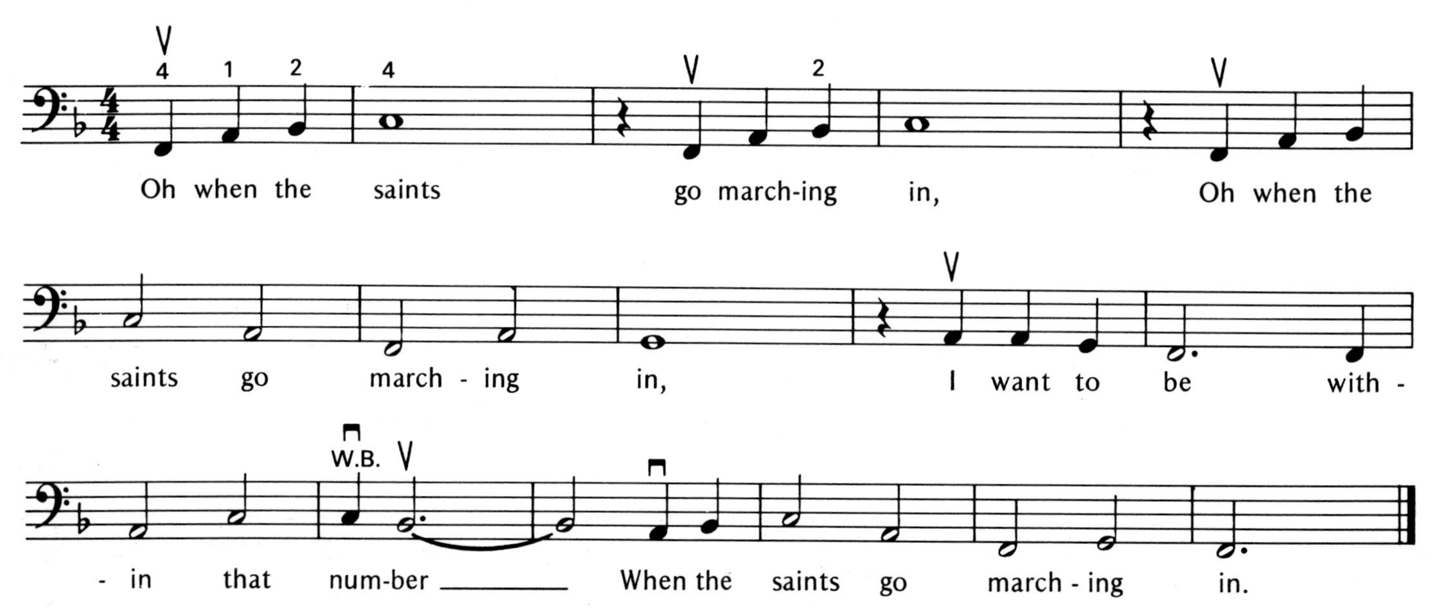

4 1 2 4 2
Oh when the saints go march-ing in, Oh when the
saints go march - ing in, I want to be with -
W.B.
- in that num-ber When the saints go march - ing in.

32 Shepherds' call

French folk song

33 Thank U very much

Michael McGear

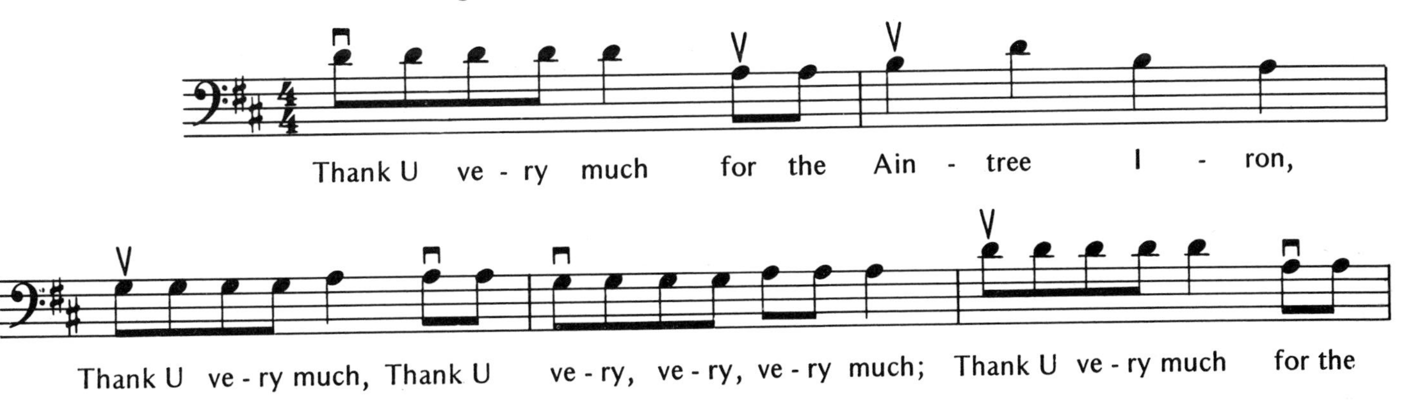
Thank U ve - ry much for the Ain - tree I - ron,
Thank U ve - ry much, Thank U ve - ry, ve - ry, ve - ry much; Thank U ve - ry much for the

Ain - tree I - ron, Thank U ve - ry, ve - ry, ve - ry much.

34 Valse triste

Maja Passchier

Slowly and smoothly
mp
(TEACHER)
mf
rit.
a tempo
mp

35 Hush-a-bye, baby

traditional

= 'zig-zag' ⊓ V ⊓ using the whole bow.
= 'zig-zag' V ⊓ V using the whole bow.

p
Hush - a - bye ba - by on the tree - top. When the wind
blows the cra - dle will rock. When the bough breaks the
cra - dle will fall; Down will come ba - by, cra - dle and all.

36 Dance of the cuckoos

Marvin Hatley

37 Bobby Shafto

traditional

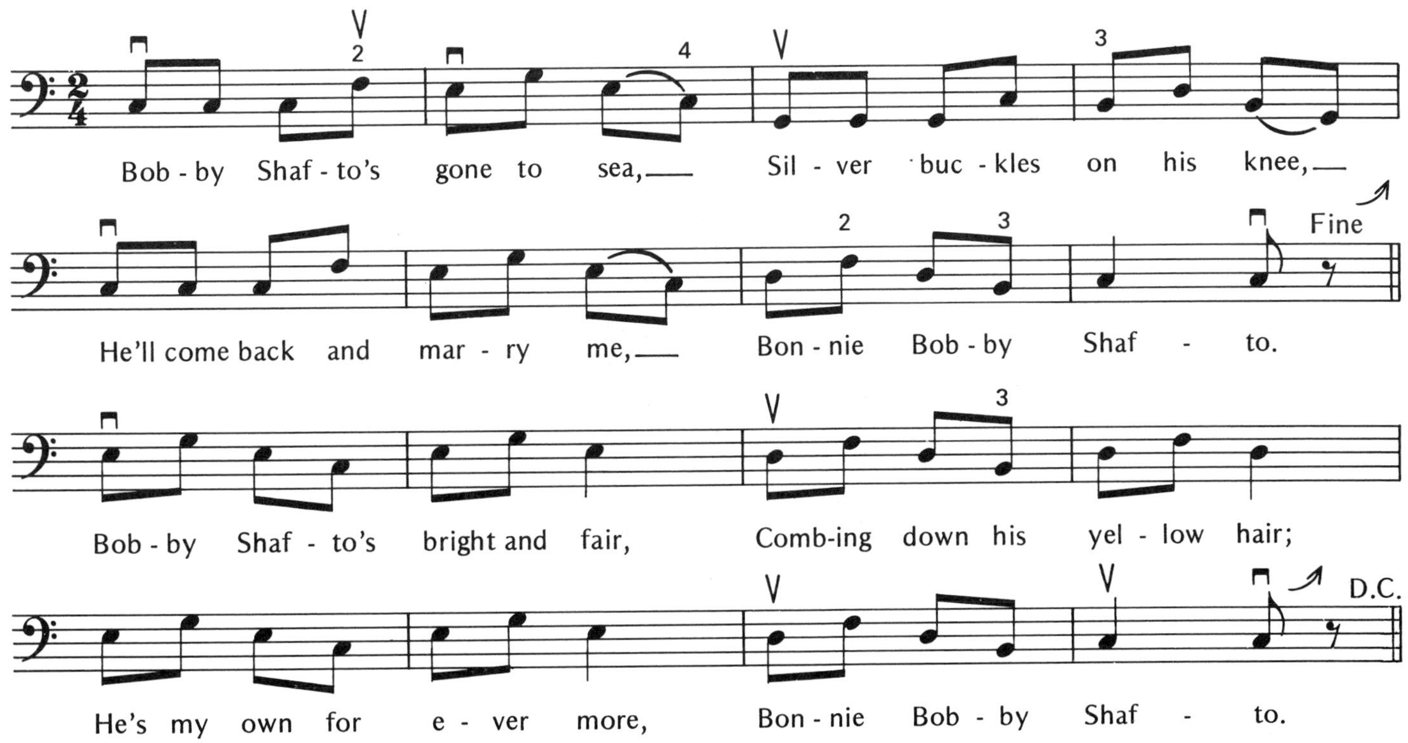
Bob - by Shaf - to's gone to sea, Sil - ver buc - kles on his knee,
Fine
He'll come back and mar - ry me, Bon - nie Bob - by Shaf - to.
Bob - by Shaf - to's bright and fair, Comb-ing down his yel - low hair;
D.C.
He's my own for e - ver more, Bon - nie Bob - by Shaf - to.

38 Can-can

Offenbach

= keep the finger on the string.

39 Song of the Delhi tongawallah

words: English version by Getsie Samuel
music: Hindustani folk song

A dot over or under a note indicates that it is to be played staccato – that is, short and detached, with the bow on the string.

Gal-lop quick-ly, gal-lop quick-ly, Gal-lop quick-ly, bro-ther horse. Gal-lop quick-ly,
gal - lop quick - ly, Gal-lop quick - ly bro - ther horse. We have still five
Fine
miles of trav - 'ling And the shades of night are fal - ling.
D.C.

40 Abracadabra staccato

Philip Clarke

Vivo
pizz.
(TEACHER)

41 Kum ba yah
African
Andante
mp
Kum ba yah, my Lord, kum ba yah,
p
Kum ba yah, my Lord, kum ba yah,
mp
Kum ba yah, my Lord, kum ba yah, Oh Lord, kum ba yah.
42 The grand old Duke of York
traditional
Oh, the grand old Duke of York, He had ten thou-sand men.
He marched them up to the top of the hill And he marched them down a - gain.
And when they were up they were up. And when they were down they were down.
And when they were on - ly half way up they were nei - ther up nor down.

43 Puff the magic dragon

Peter Yarrow/Leonard Lipton

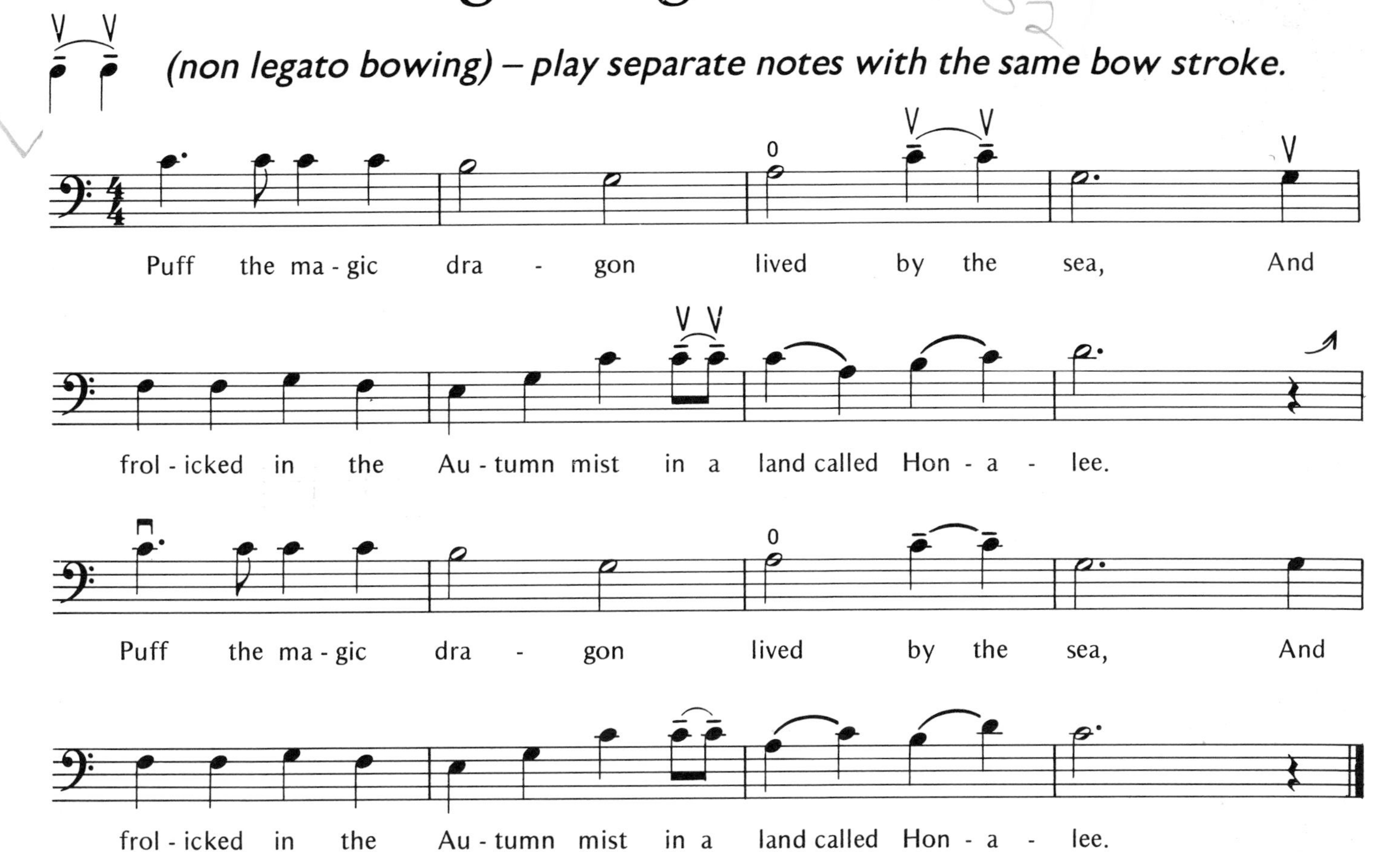
(non legato bowing) – play separate notes with the same bow stroke.
Puff the ma-gic dra-gon lived by the sea, And
frol-icked in the Au-tumn mist in a land called Hon-a-lee.
Puff the ma-gic dra-gon lived by the sea, And
frol-icked in the Au-tumn mist in a land called Hon-a-lee.

44 Three blind mice

traditional

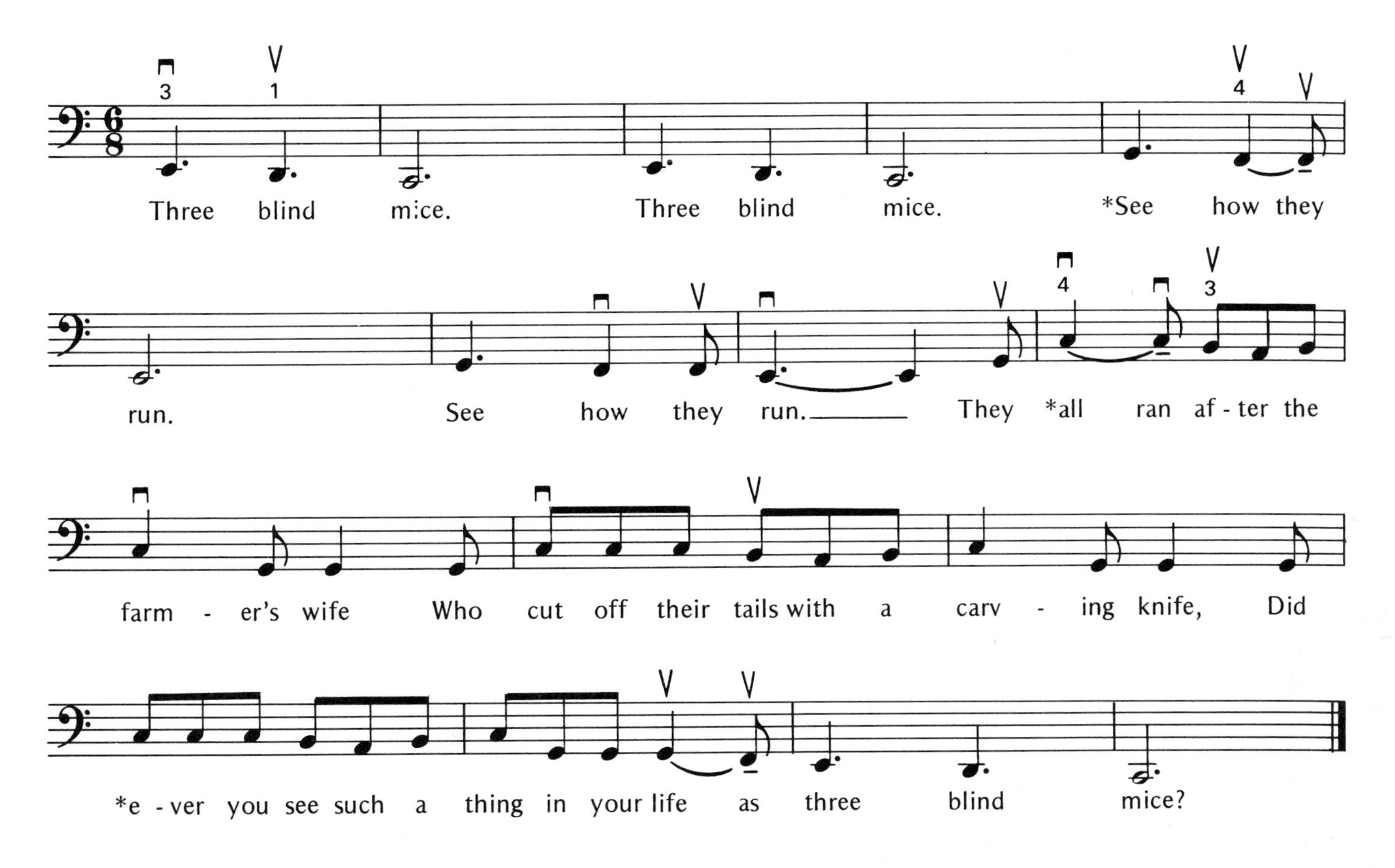
Three blind mice. Three blind mice. *See how they
run. See how they run. They *all ran af-ter the
farm-er's wife Who cut off their tails with a carv-ing knife, Did
*e-ver you see such a thing in your life as three blind mice?

*entry point when played as a round

45 Hickory dickory dock

traditional

Hick - o - ry dick - o - ry dock! The mouse ran up the
clock. The clock struck one, the mouse ran down. Hick-o - ry dick - o - ry dock.

46 My love is like a red, red rose

traditional Scottish

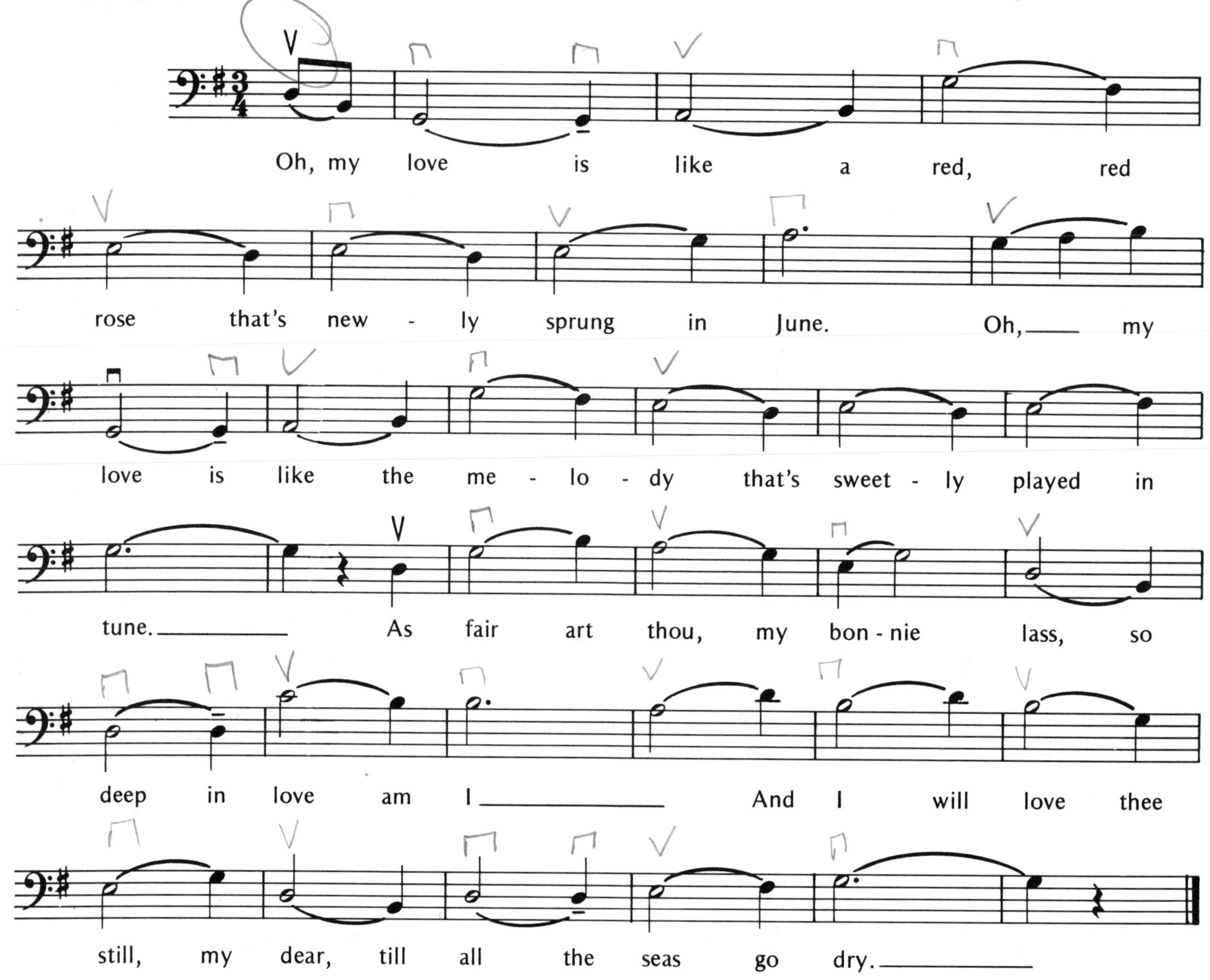
Oh, my love is like a red, red
rose that's new - ly sprung in June. Oh, my
love is like the me - lo - dy that's sweet - ly played in
tune. As fair art thou, my bon - nie lass, so
deep in love am I And I will love thee
still, my dear, till all the seas go dry.

47 Whose pigs are these?

traditional

Whose pigs are these? *Whose pigs are these? They

*are John Potts', I can tell 'em by the spots And I *found'em in the vi-car - age gar - den.

*entry point when played as a round

48 Berceuse d'Auvergne

French

heel = stay at the heel end of the bow.

Allegretto
point
mf
W.B.
point
p
W.B.
mf
heel

49 An Eriskay love-lilt

Mary MacInnes
Collected by Marjory Kennedy-Fraser

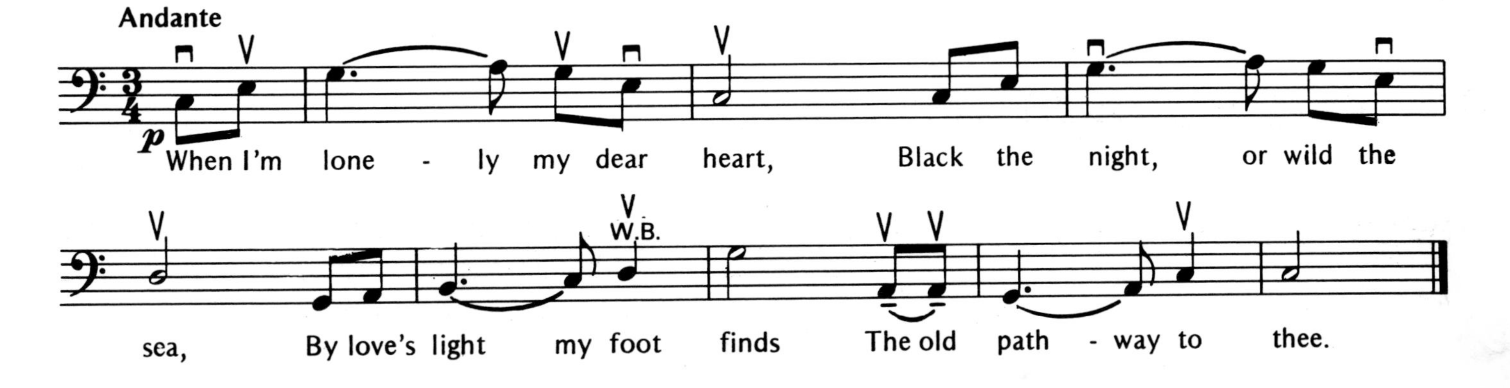
Andante
p
When I'm lone - ly my dear heart, Black the night, or wild the
W.B.
sea, By love's light my foot finds The old path - way to thee.

50 Clementine

traditional

Oh my dar - ling, Oh my dar - ling, Oh my dar - ling Clem - en -
tine, Thou art lost and gone for - e - ver, Dread-ful sor - ry Clem-en - tine.

51 Jingle bells

traditional

Allegretto
Jin - gle bells, jin - gle bells, jin - gle all the way! Oh what fun it
is to ride in a one - horse o - pen sleigh. Oh! Jin - gle bells, jin - gle bells,
jin - gle all the way! Oh what fun it is to ride in a one-horse o - pen sleigh.

52 The drunken sailor

traditional

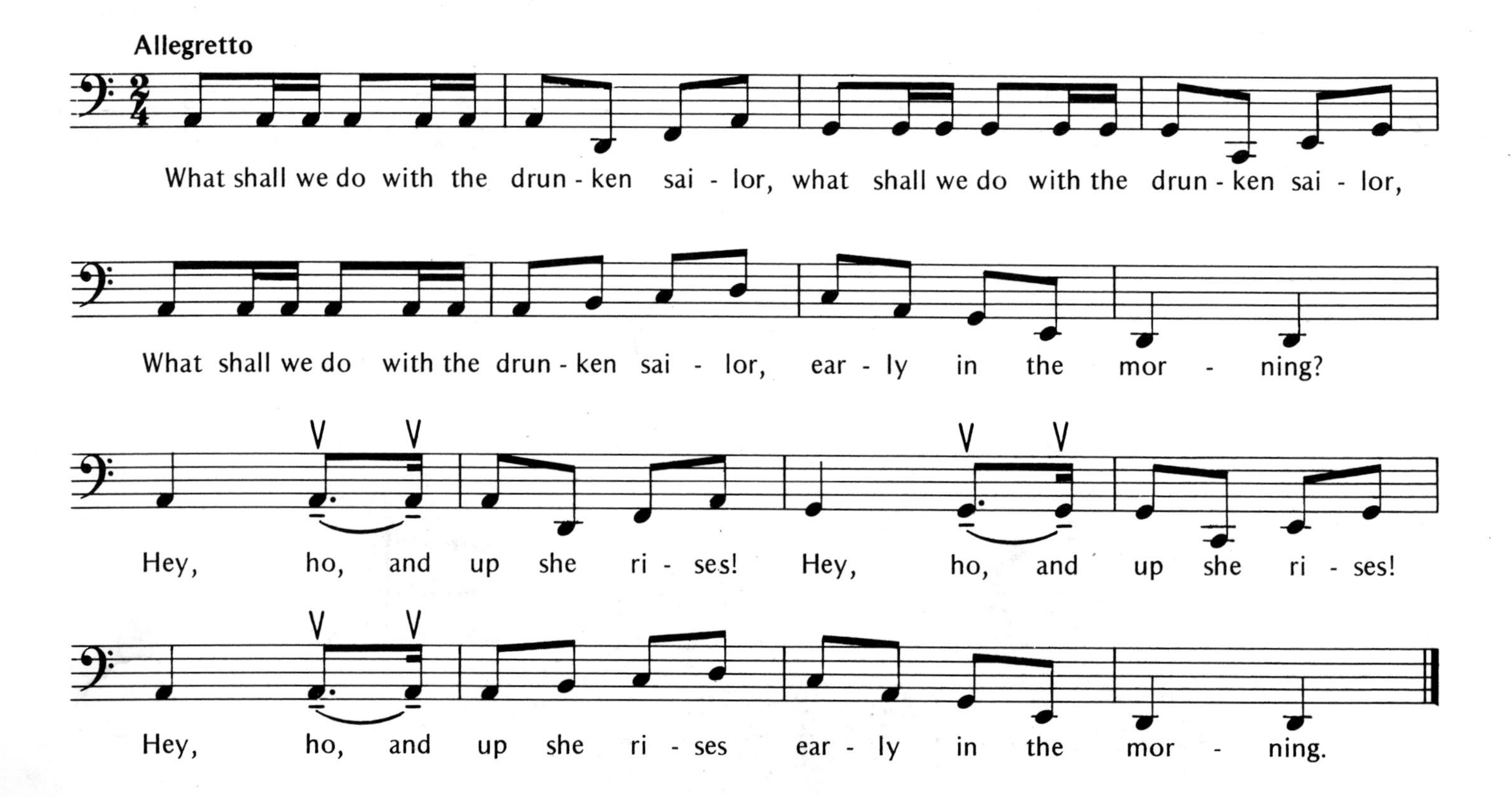
Allegretto
What shall we do with the drun - ken sai - lor, what shall we do with the drun - ken sai - lor,
What shall we do with the drun - ken sai - lor, ear - ly in the mor - ning?
Hey, ho, and up she ri - ses! Hey, ho, and up she ri - ses!
Hey, ho, and up she ri - ses ear - ly in the mor - ning.

53 Hey, Betty Martin

North American

Hey Bet - ty Mar - tin, tip - py toe, tip - py toe, Hey Bet - ty Mar - tin,
tip - toe fine. Hey Bet - ty Mar - tin, tip - py toe, tip-py toe, Hey Bet-ty Mar - tin,
Fine
please be mine. Swing with me, I'll swing with you, We'll go swing-ing the
D.C.
whole day through. Swing so fast, swing so fine, swing-ing, swing-ing all the time.

54 MacPherson's farewell

words: Robert Burns
music: traditional

Allegro ma non troppo
mf
Fare - well, ye dun - geons dark__ and__ strong, The__ wretch - 's des - tin -
- ie! Mac - Pher - son's time will not be long, On yon - der gal - lows-
cresc.
- tree. Sae__ rant - ing - ly, sae__ wan - ton - ly, Sae__ daun - ting - ly__ gae'd
f
he: He played a spring, and__ danc'd it round Be - low the gal - lows - tree.

55 Polly-wolly-doodle

traditional

Oh my Sal she am a maid-en fair, Sing-ing Pol - ly - wol - ly - doo-dle all the
day. With laugh - ing eyes and curl - y hair Sing
Pol-ly-wol-ly - doo-dle all the day. Fare thee well, Fare thee well, Fare thee
well my fai - ry fay. Oh I'm off to Louis - i - an - na for to
see my Su - sy An - na, Sing-ing Pol - ly - wol - ly - doo - dle all the day.

56 Here we go round the mulberry bush

traditional

Here we go round the mul - berry bush, the mul - berry bush, the mul - berry bush.
Here we go round the mul - berry bush on a cold and frost - y morn - ing.

57 Row, row, row the boat

traditional

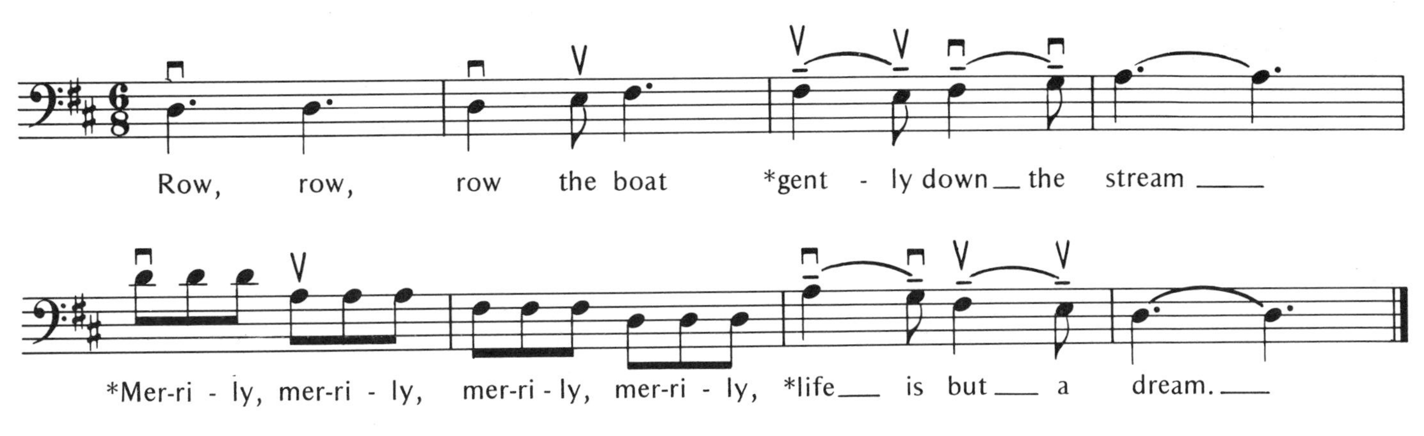
Row, row, row the boat *gent - ly down __ the stream ____
*Mer-ri - ly, mer-ri - ly, mer-ri - ly, mer-ri - ly, *life __ is but __ a dream. ____

*entry point when played as a round

58 Land of the silver birch

Canadian Indian canoeing song

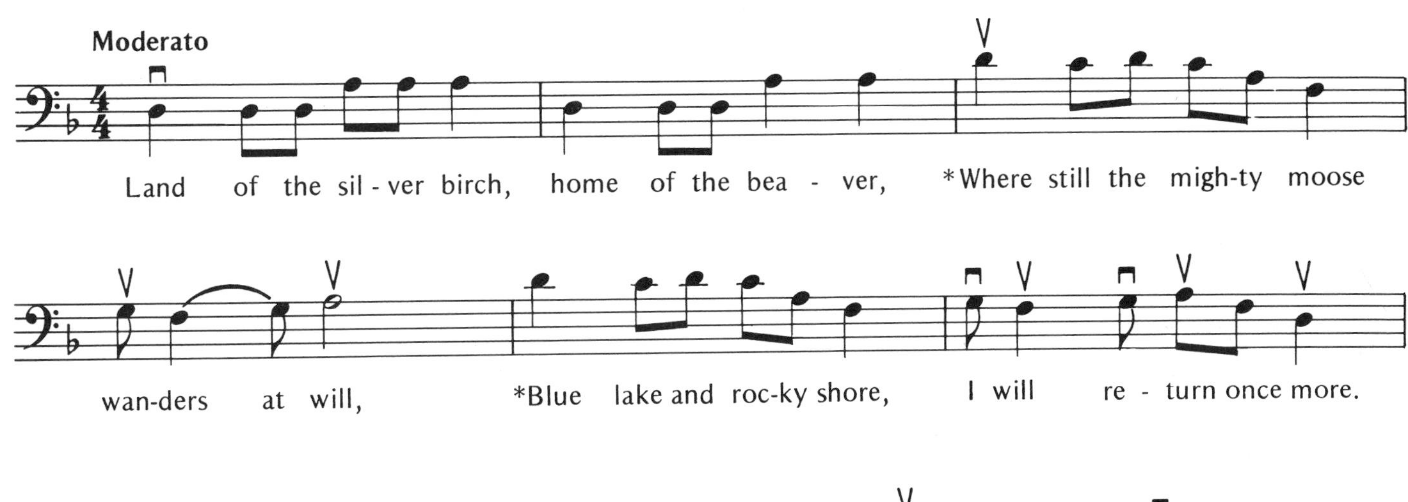
Moderato
Land of the sil - ver birch, home of the bea - ver, *Where still the migh-ty moose
wan-ders at will, *Blue lake and roc-ky shore, I will re - turn once more.

*Hi hi-ya hi - ya, hi hi-ya hi - ya, hi - hi - ya hi - ya hi - - - ya.

*entry point when played as a round

59 Oranges and lemons

traditional

2
mf
Or - ang-es and le - mons say the bells of St Clem-ent's. I owe you five

Fine
far - things say the bells of St Mar - tin's.
f
When will you pay me say the

D.C.
bells of Old Bai - ley. When I grow rich say the bells of Shore - ditch.

60 Kol dōdi

traditional Hebrew

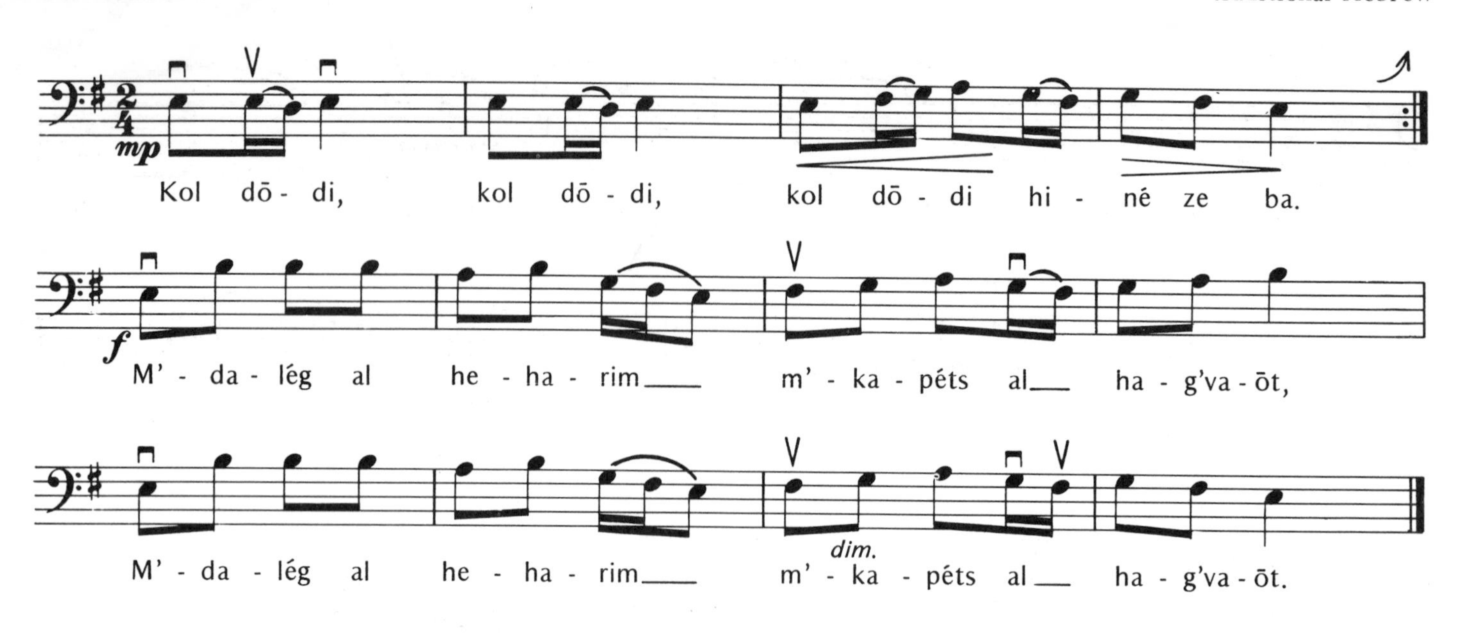
mp
Kol dō - di, kol dō - di, kol dō - di hi - né ze ba.
f
M' - da - lég al he - ha - rim m' - ka - péts al ha - g'va - ōt,
dim.
M' - da - lég al he - ha - rim m' - ka - péts al ha - g'va - ōt.

61 Scarborough Fair

English folk song

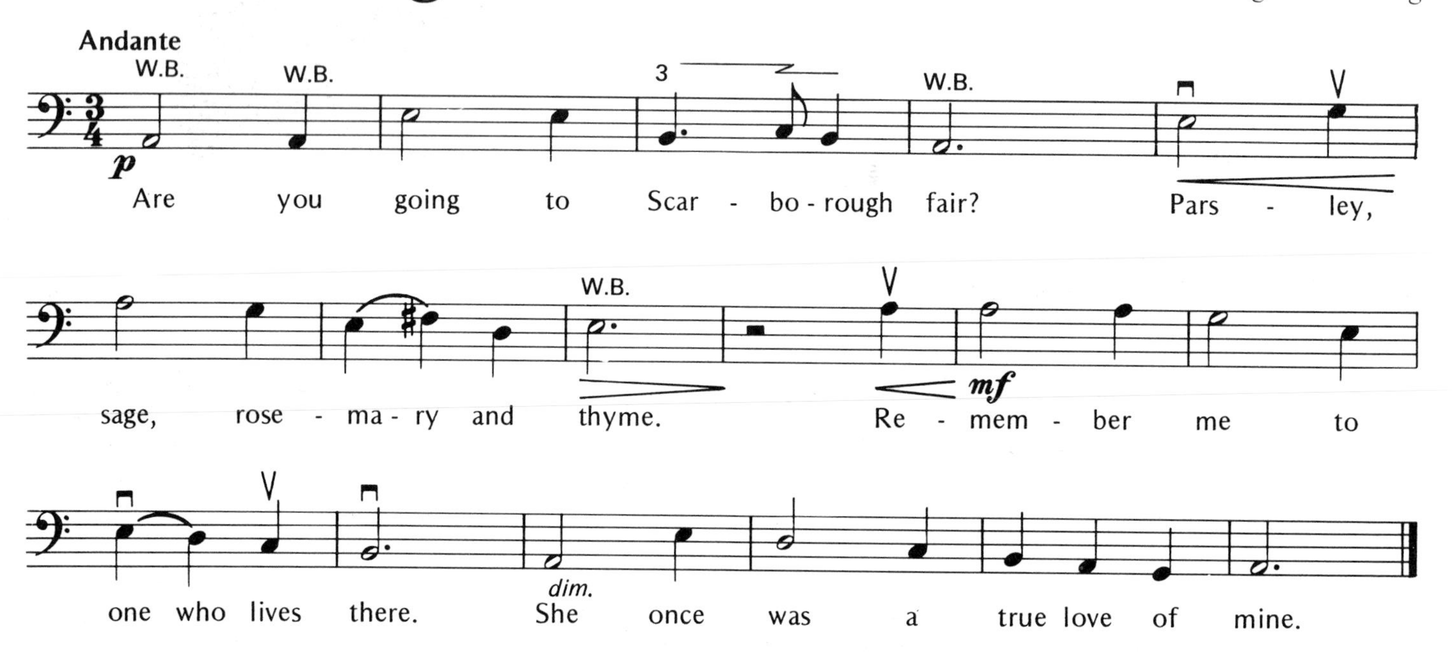
Andante
W.B.
W.B.
3
W.B.
p
Are you going to Scar - bo - rough fair? Pars - ley,
W.B.
mf
sage, rose - ma - ry and thyme. Re - mem - ber me to
dim.
one who lives there. She once was a true love of mine.

62 Winds through the olive trees

traditional French

2
mp
Winds through the o - live trees soft - ly did blow Round lit - tle
p
Beth - le-hem, long long a - go. Sheep on the hill - side lay
mp
white as the snow, Shep-herds were watch -ing them, Long, long a - go.

63 Plaisir d'amour
G P Martini
Andante
Plai - sir d'a - mour ne du - re qu'un mo - ment, Cha -
- grin d'a - mour du-re toute la vie.
64 All my loving
Lennon/McCartney
Close your eyes and I'll kiss you, To - mor - row I'll
point
miss you; Re - mem - ber I'll al - ways be true. And then
while I'm a - way, I'll write home ev - 'ry day, And I'll send all my
W.B.
lov - ing to you All my lov - ing I will send to
you, All my lov - ing, dar-ling, I'll be true.

65 Over the hills and far away

traditional

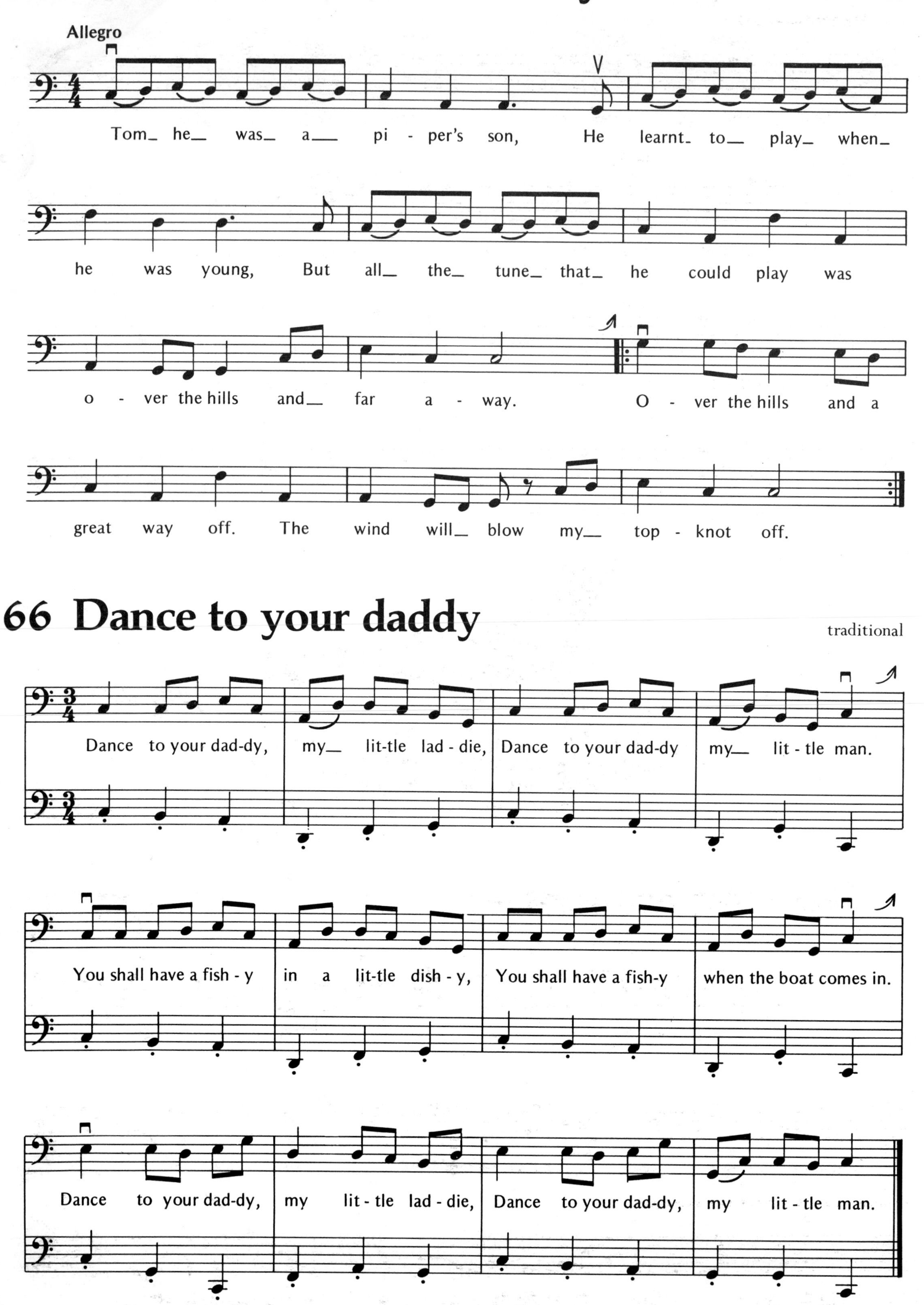
Allegro
Tom_ he_ was_ a_ pi - per's son, He learnt_ to_ play_ when_
he was young, But all_ the_ tune_ that_ he could play was
o - ver the hills and_ far a - way. O - ver the hills and a
great way off. The wind will_ blow my_ top - knot off.
66 Dance to your daddy
traditional
Dance to your dad-dy, my_ lit-tle lad - die, Dance to your dad-dy my_ lit - tle man.
You shall have a fish - y in a lit-tle dish - y, You shall have a fish-y when the boat comes in.
Dance to your dad-dy, my lit - tle lad - die, Dance to your dad-dy, my lit - tle man.

67 Morningtown ride

Malvina Reynolds

Allegro moderato
point
W.B.
point
mp
Train whis - tle blow - ing Makes a sleep - y noise.
W.B.
point
Un - der - neath their blan - kets Go all the girls and boys.
W.B.
Rock - ing, roll - ing, rid - ing, out a - long the bay.
All bound for Morn-ing - town, ma-ny miles a - way.

68 Morning has broken

words: Eleanor Farjeon
music: Gaelic

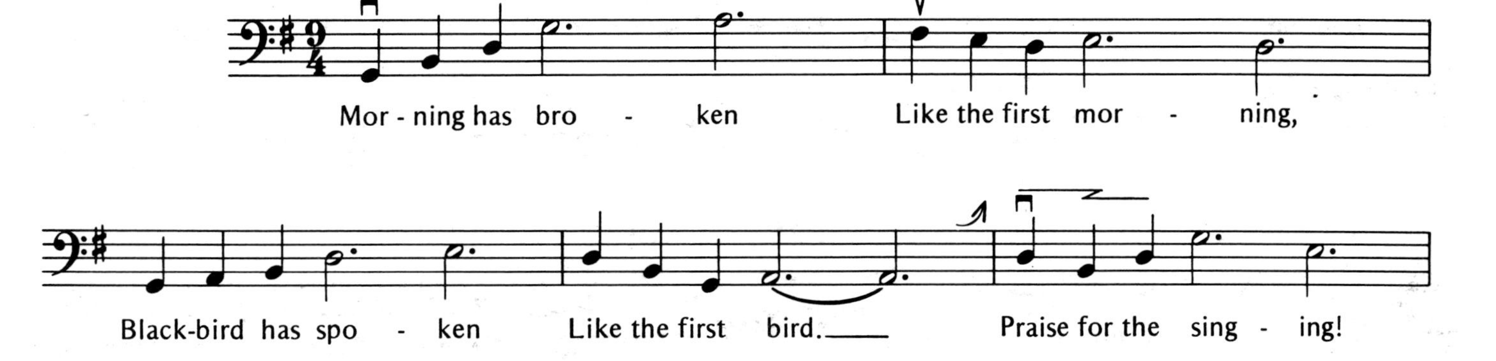
Mor - ning has bro - ken Like the first mor - ning,
Black-bird has spo - ken Like the first bird.___ Praise for the sing - ing!

Praise for the mor - ning! Praise for them, spring - ing, Fresh from the Word!___

FIRST EXTENSION – first finger extended back.
X = extension between first and second fingers.

69 Portsmouth

traditional

70 Apusski dusky

traditional

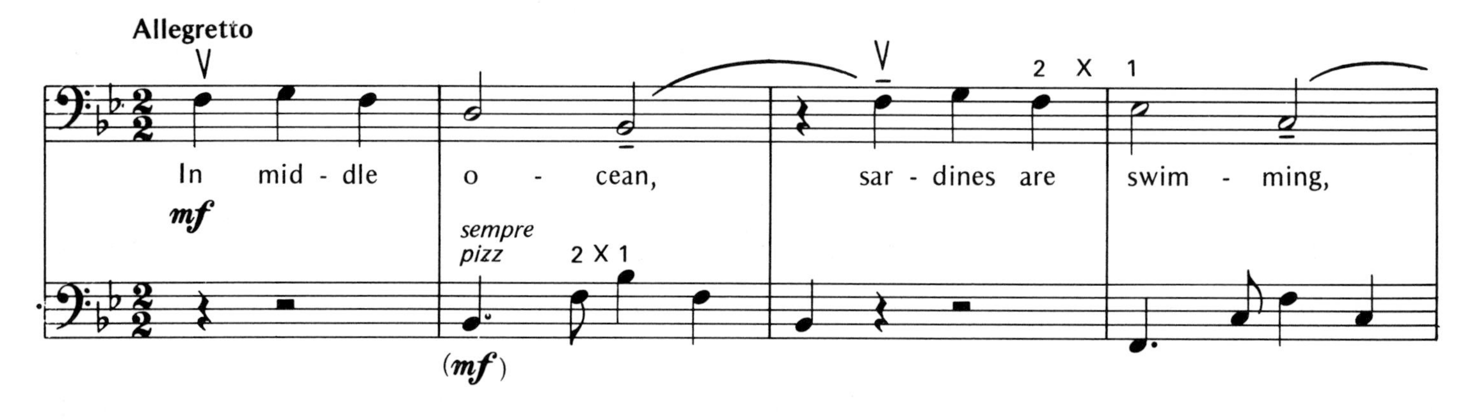
Allegretto
In mid - dle o - cean, sar - dines are swim - ming,
mf
sempre pizz
(mf)

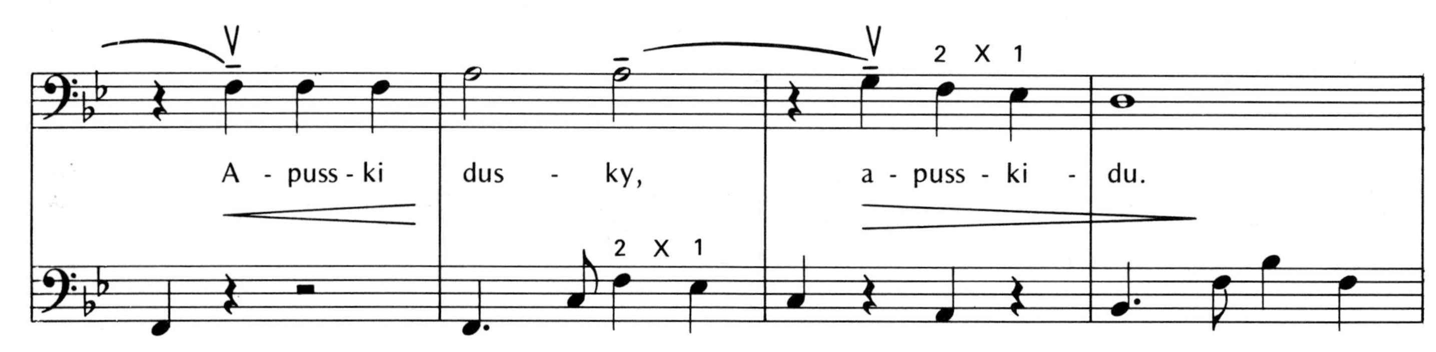
A - puss - ki dus - ky, a - puss - ki - du.

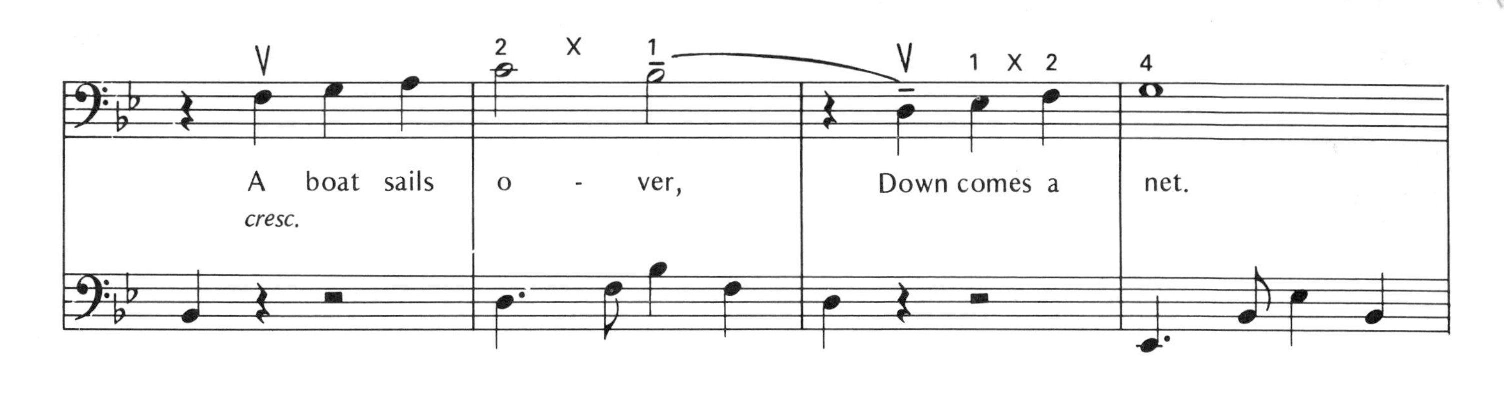
A boat sails o - ver, Down comes a net.
cresc.

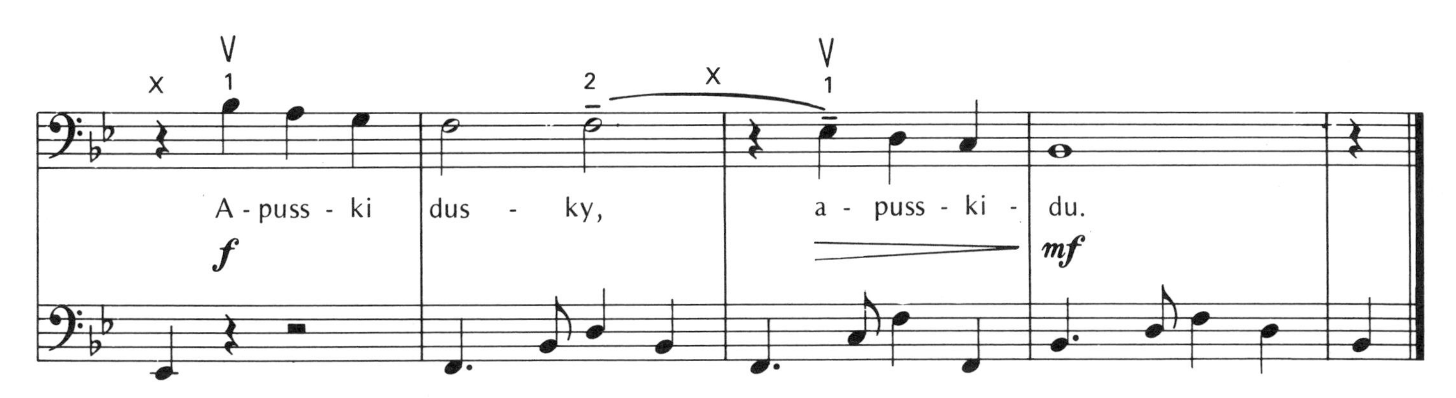
A - puss - ki dus - ky, a - puss - ki - du.
f
mf

71 In dulci jubilo

words: trans P Dearmer
music: 14th century German

In dul - ci ju - bi - lo Now sing with
hearts a - glow. Our de - light and
plea - sure lies in prae - se - pi - o,
Like sun - shine is our trea - sure Ma
tris in gre - mi - o. Al - pha
es et O, Al - pha es et O.

72 Shalom

traditional Hebrew

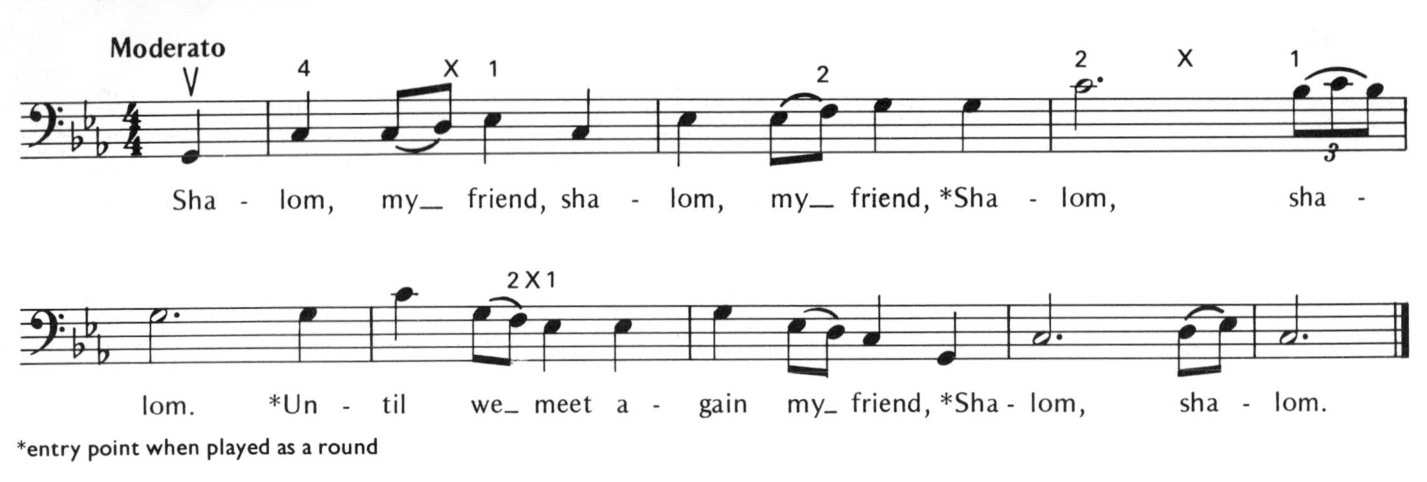
Moderato
Sha - lom, my_ friend, sha - lom, my_ friend, *Sha - lom, sha -
lom. *Un - til we_ meet a - gain my_ friend, *Sha - lom, sha - lom.

*entry point when played as a round

73 Away in a manger

W J Kirkpatrick

A - way in a_ man - ger, no_ crib for a

bed, The_ lit - tle Lord Je - sus laid_ down his sweet

head, The stars in the_ bright sky looked_ down where he

lay. The_ lit - tle Lord Je - sus a - sleep on the hay.

74 Theme from 'Kol nidrei'

Max Bruch

Adagio ma non troppo
dolce
cresc.

75 Whip jamboree

traditional

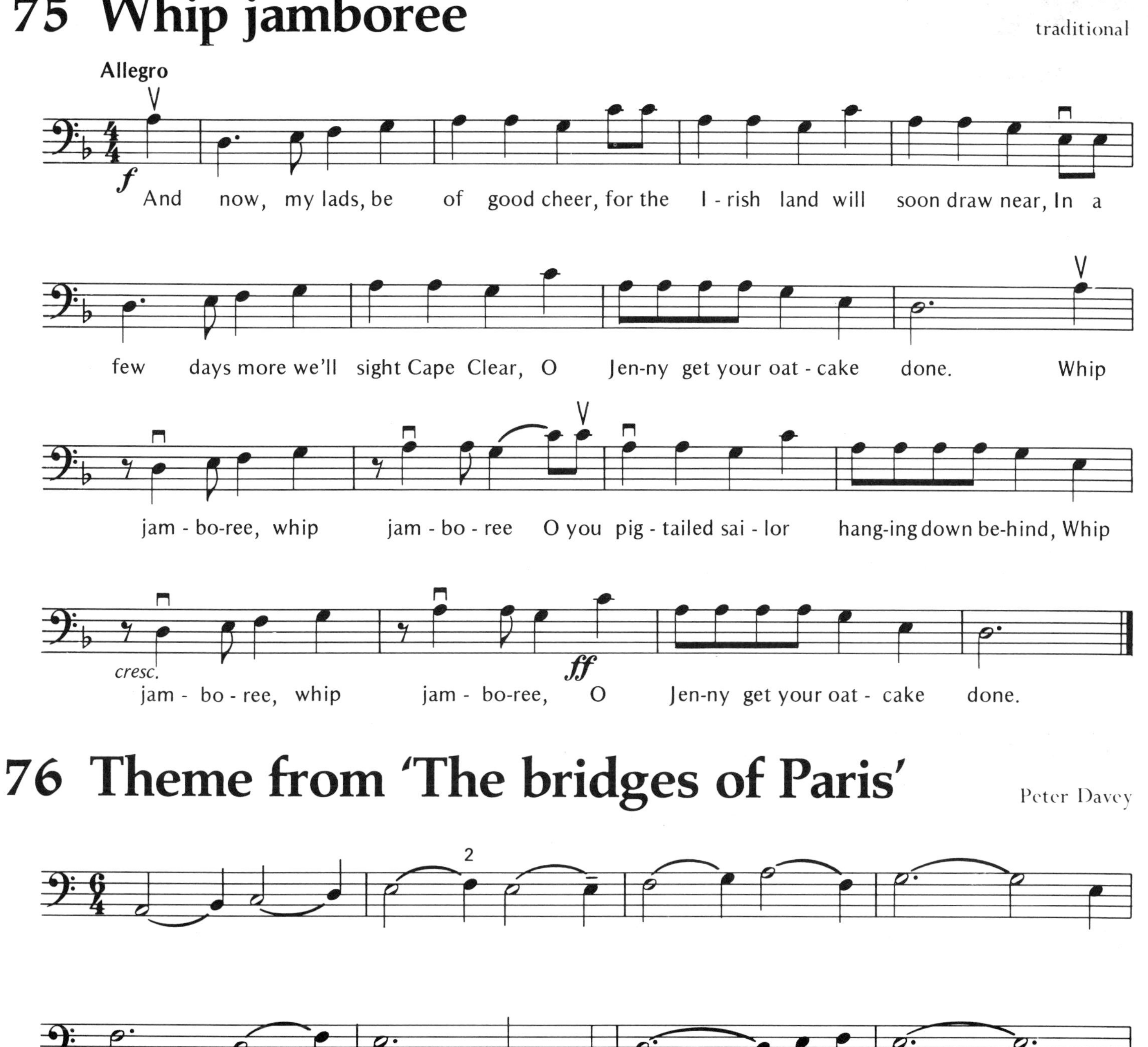
Allegro
f
And now, my lads, be of good cheer, for the I - rish land will soon draw near, In a
few days more we'll sight Cape Clear, O Jen-ny get your oat - cake done. Whip
jam - bo-ree, whip jam - bo - ree O you pig - tailed sai - lor hang-ing down be-hind, Whip
cresc.
jam - bo - ree, whip jam - bo-ree, O Jen-ny get your oat - cake done.
ff

76 Theme from 'The bridges of Paris'

Peter Davey

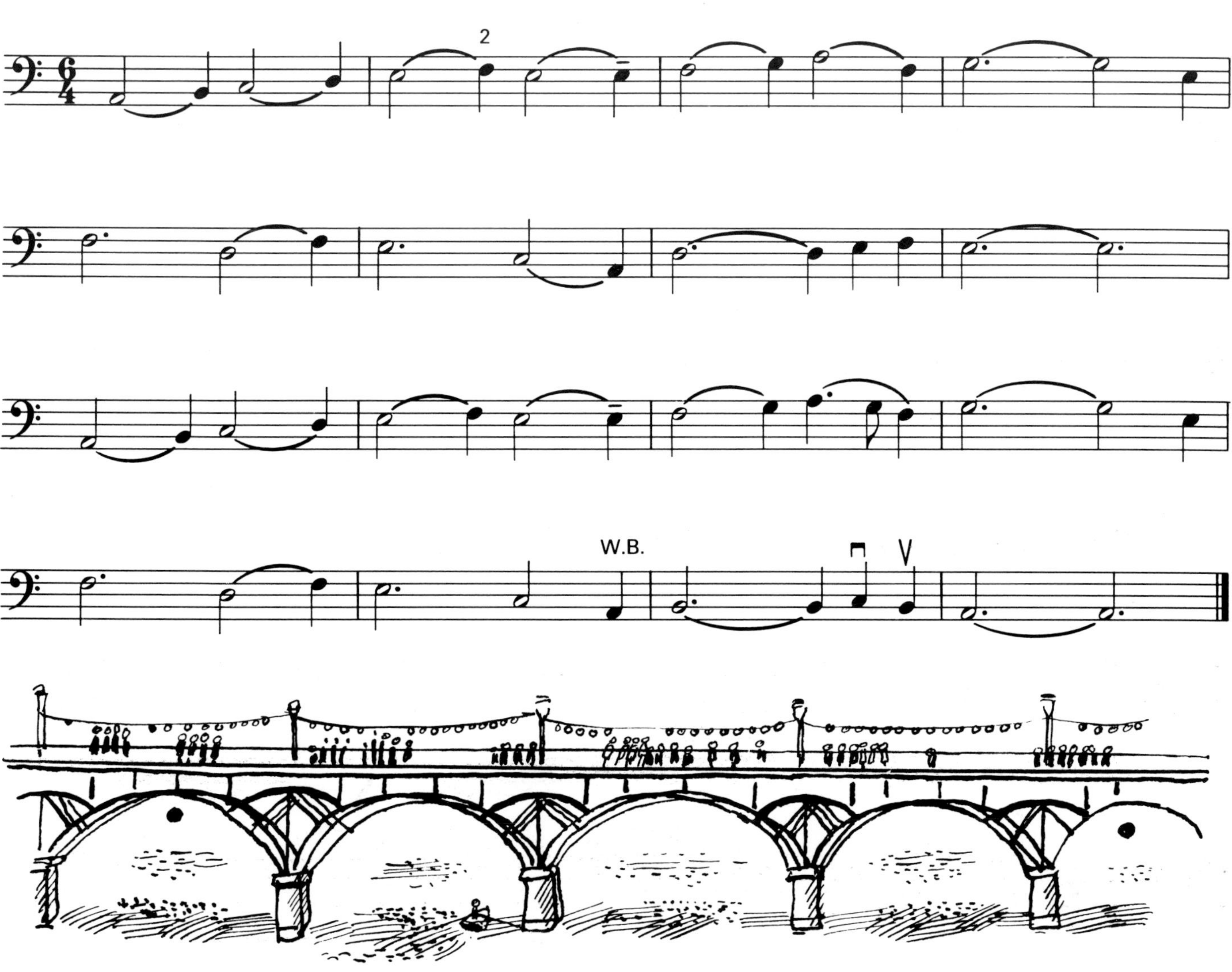
2
W.B.

77 Water come a me eye

Jamaican

Quite fast
Ev - 'ry time I re - mem - ber Li - za, wa - ter come a me eye.

When I think a - bout my gal Li - za wa - ter come a me eye.

Come back Li - za, come back gal, Wa - ter come a me eye.

Come back Li - za, come back gal, Wa - ter come a me eye.

78 Andantino

Beethoven

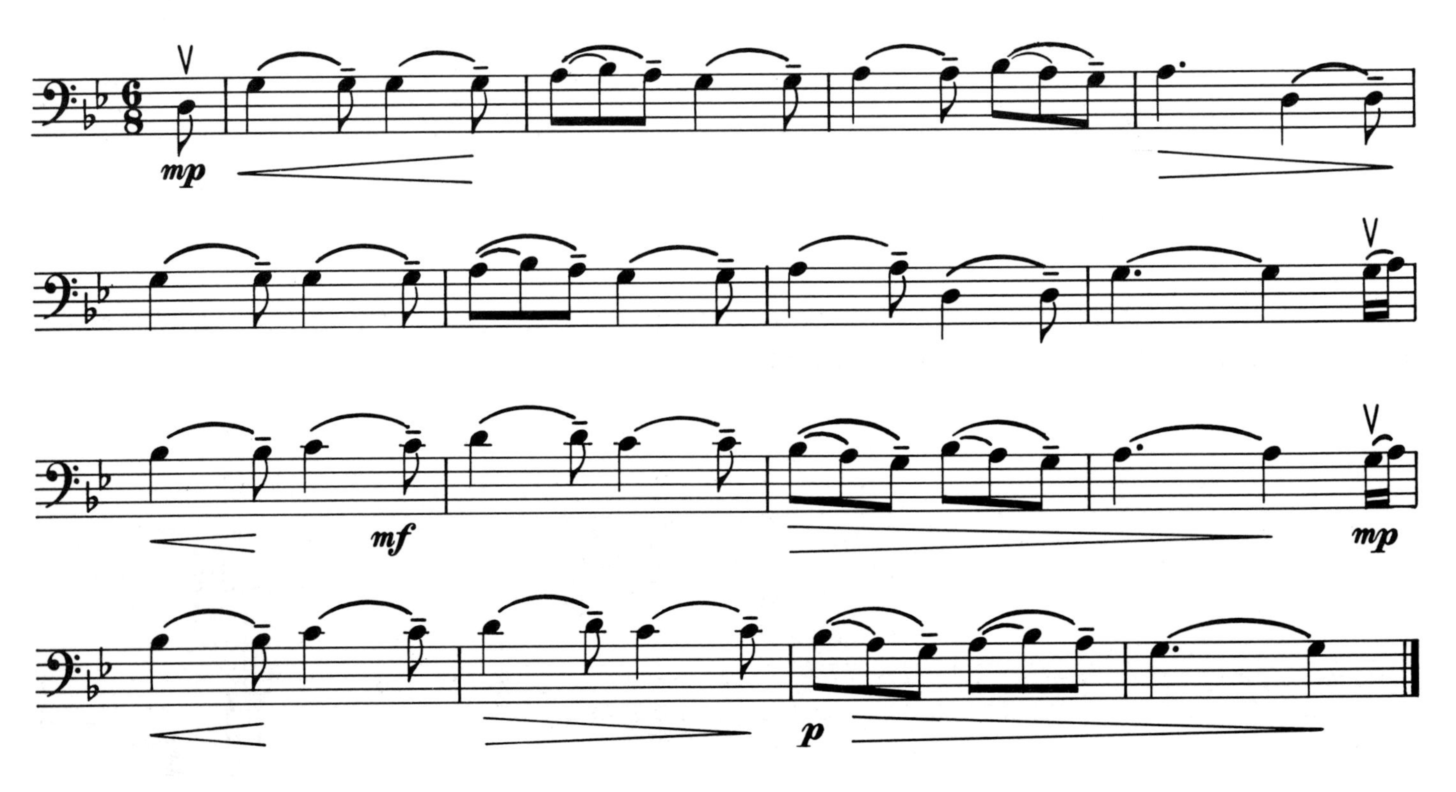
mp
mf
mp
p

79 Give me oil in my lamp

traditional

W.B.
Give me oil in my lamp, keep me burn - ing, give me
oil in my lamp, I pray. Give me oil in my lamp, keep me
W.B.
burn - ing, Keep me burn-ing till the break of day. Sing ho - san - na,
sing ho - san - na, sing ho - san - na to the King of Kings.
Sing ho - san - na, sing ho - san - na, sing ho - san-na to the King.

SECOND EXTENSION – moving the thumb + second, third and fourth fingers forwards over the interval of a semitone.

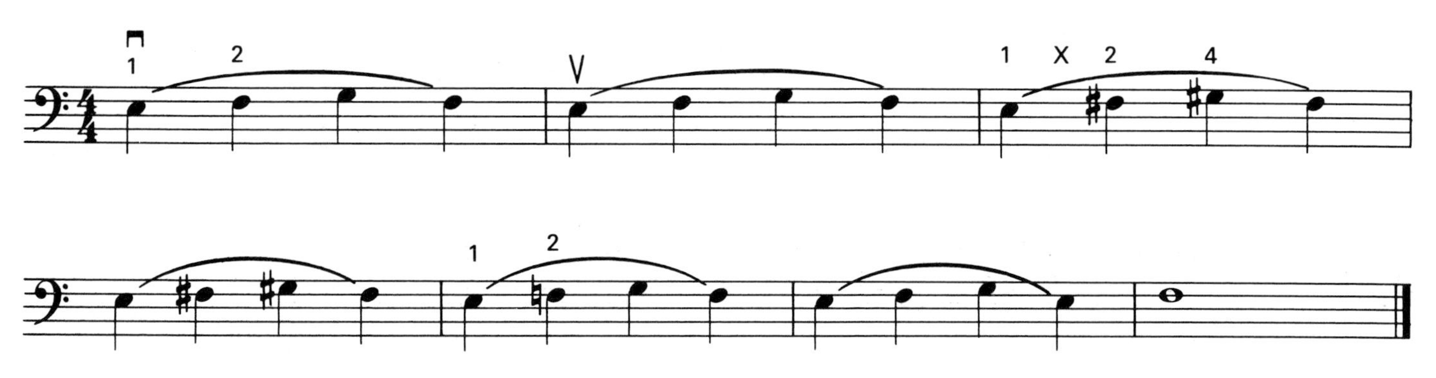

80 Deck the hall

traditional Welsh

Deck the hall with boughs of hol - ly, Fa - la-la-la - la, Fa - la - la - la.

'Tis the sea - son to be jol - ly, Fa - la-la-la - la, Fa - la - la - la.

Fill the mead cup, drain the bar - rel, Fa - la - la - la - la, la - la - la.

Troll the an - cient Christ-mas ca - rol, Fa-la-la-la - la, Fa - la - la - la.

81 The first Nowell

traditional

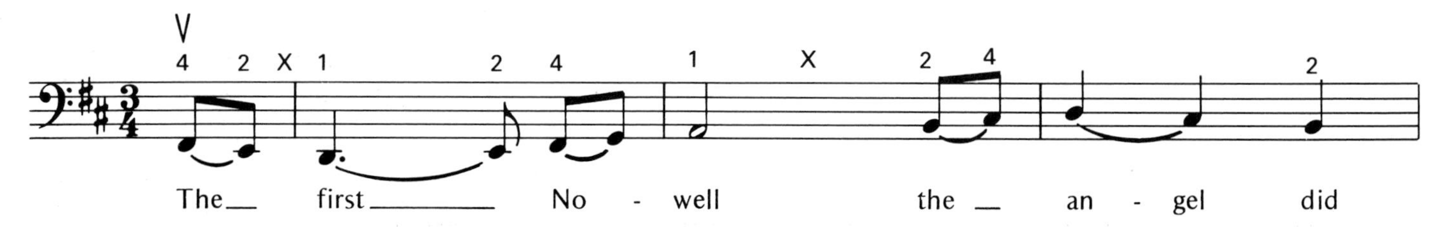
The first No - well the an - gel did

say Was to cer - tain poor shep - herds in fields as they

lay; In fields where they lay keep - ing their

sheep In a cold win - ter's night that was so

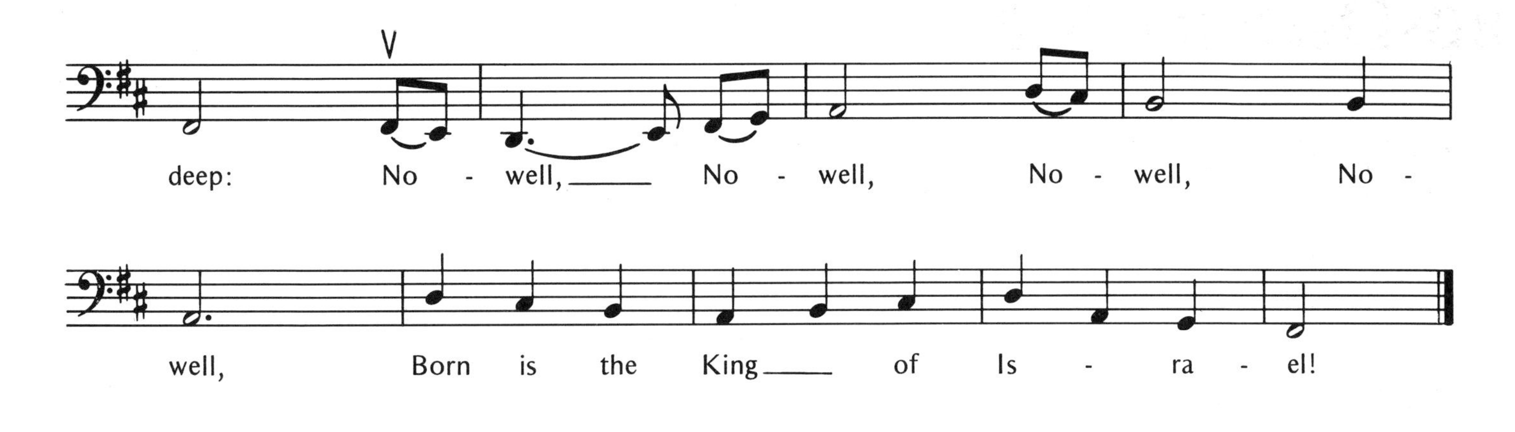
V
deep: No - well, No - well, No - well, No -
well, Born is the King of Is - ra - el!

82 Nowhere man

Lennon/McCartney

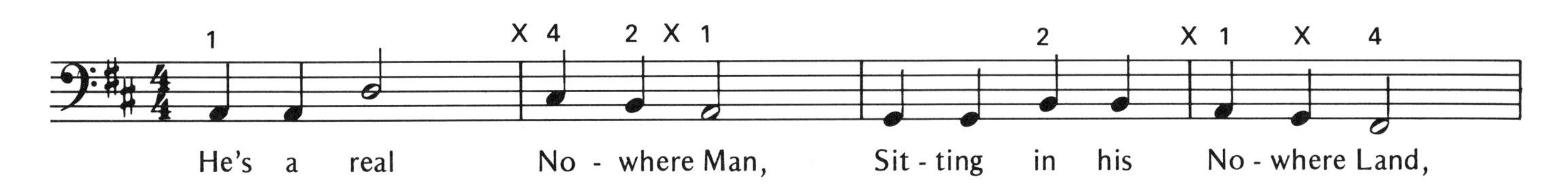
1 X 4 2 X 1 2 X 1 X 4
He's a real No - where Man, Sit - ting in his No - where Land,

2 4 2 W.B.
Ma - king all his no - where plans for no - bo - dy.

X 4 2 X 1 2 4 2
Does-n't have a point of view, Knows not where he's go - ing to, Is - n't he a

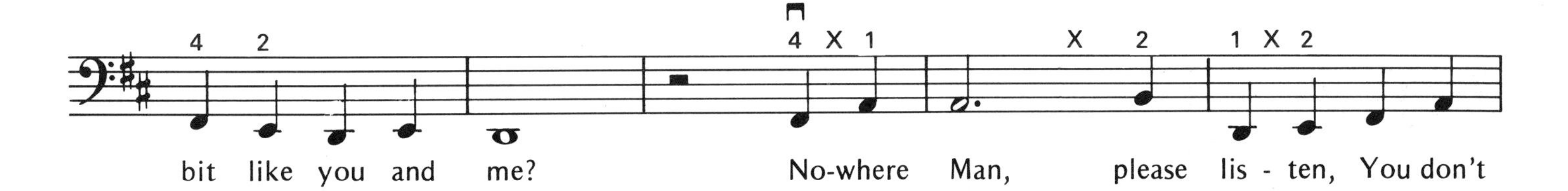
4 2 4 X 1 X 2 1 X 2
bit like you and me? No-where Man, please lis - ten, You don't

1 X 2 2 X 4 2 X1
know what you're mis - sing, No - where Man, the world is

2 2 2
at your com-mand. He's a real No - where Man, Sit - ting in his

2 X 4 2 X 1 W.B.
No-where Land, Ma - king all his no-where plans for no - bo - dy.

83 Last of the summer wine

Ronnie Hazlehurst

Andante
mp
mf

84 Porcupine's lullaby

Paul Chr Van Westering

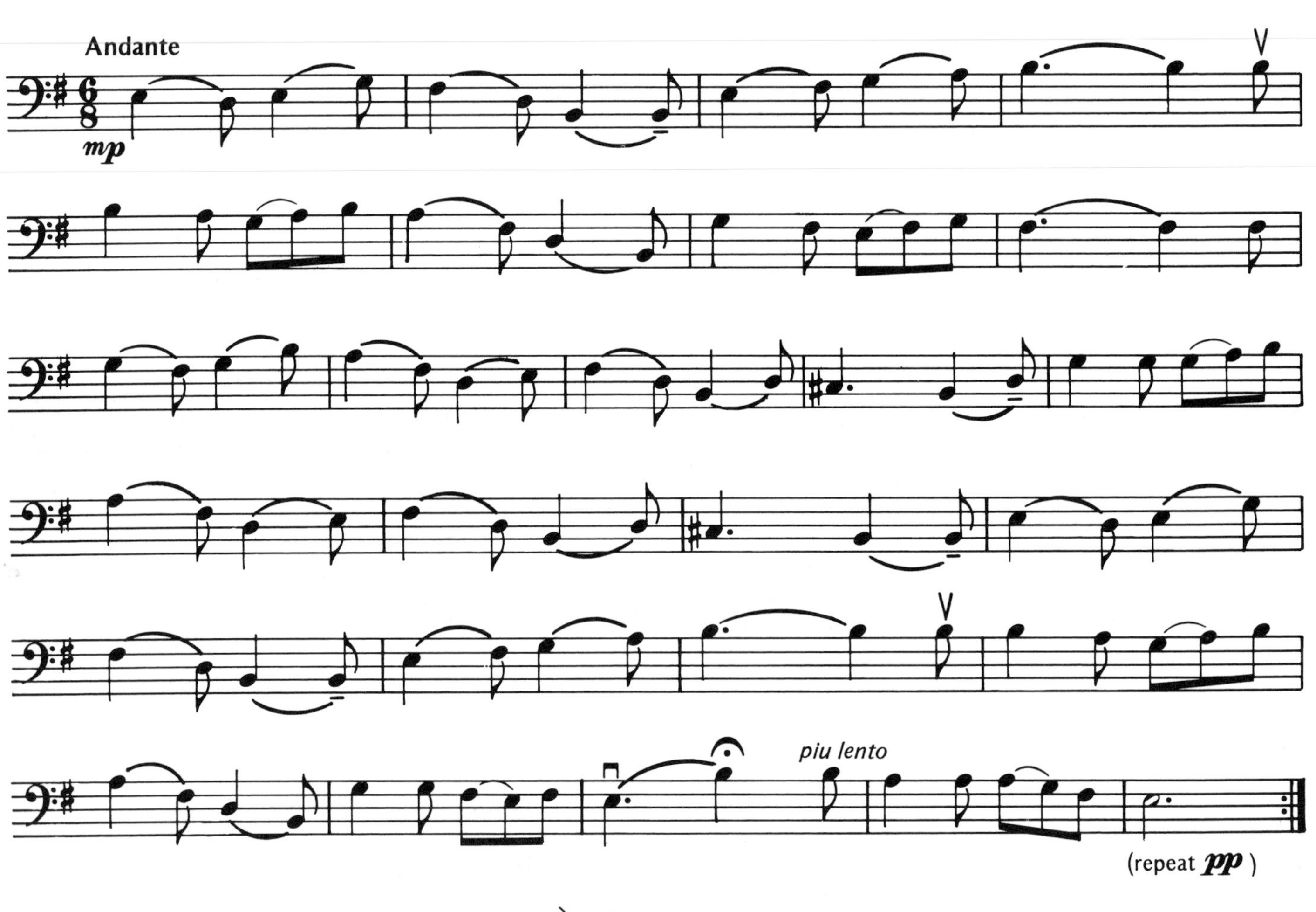
Andante
mp
piu lento
(repeat pp)

85 Silent night

words: Joseph Mohr
music: Franz Grüber

Largo
pp
Si - lent night, ho - ly night. All is calm, all is bright,
Round yon Vir - gin Mo - ther and child, Ho - ly In - fant so ten - der and mild,
p
pp
Sleep in hea - ven-ly peace,
sleep in hea - ven-ly peace.

86 Country gardens

Morris tune

f (second time mf)
f cresc.
ff
mf cresc.
f

87 Lillibullero

traditional

Allegro
88 I came from Alabama
Stephen Foster
I came from Al - a - bam - a With my ban - jo on my knee; I'm
going to Loui - si - an - a, My true love for to see. It rained all night the

day I left, The wea-ther it was dry, The sun so hot I froze to death, Su -
- san - na, don't you cry. Oh, Su - san - na, Oh don't you cry for
me, I've come from Al - a - bam - a With my ban - jo on my knee.

89 March of the kings

traditional French

90 Waltz

Mozart

91 French medley

ALOUETTE
AUPRES DE MA BLONDE

92 Skye boat song

traditional Scottish

Fine
D.C.

93 The birdcatcher's song

Mozart

Allegretto
mf
f
mf
p
mf
pp
mf

94 Go, tell it on the mountain

spiritual

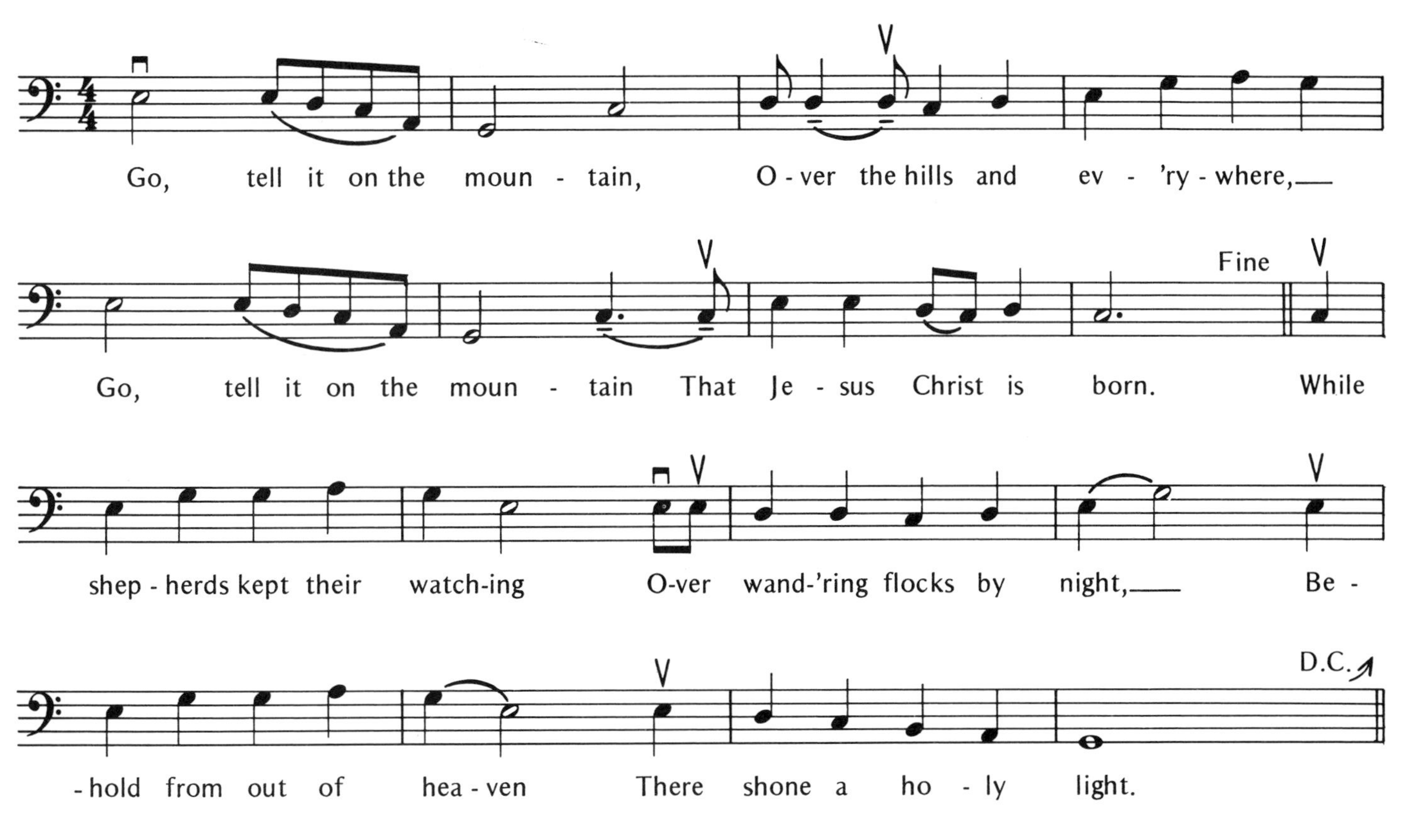
Go, tell it on the moun - tain, O - ver the hills and ev - 'ry - where,
Go, tell it on the moun - tain That Je - sus Christ is born.
Fine
While shep - herds kept their watch-ing O-ver wand-'ring flocks by night, Be -
- hold from out of hea - ven There shone a ho - ly light.
D.C.

95 Sarona

traditional Scottish

96 St Anthony chorale

Haydn (attributed)

Allegretto
mf (second time p)
p
cresc.
mf
f
dim.
p

97 Loch Lomond

traditional Scottish

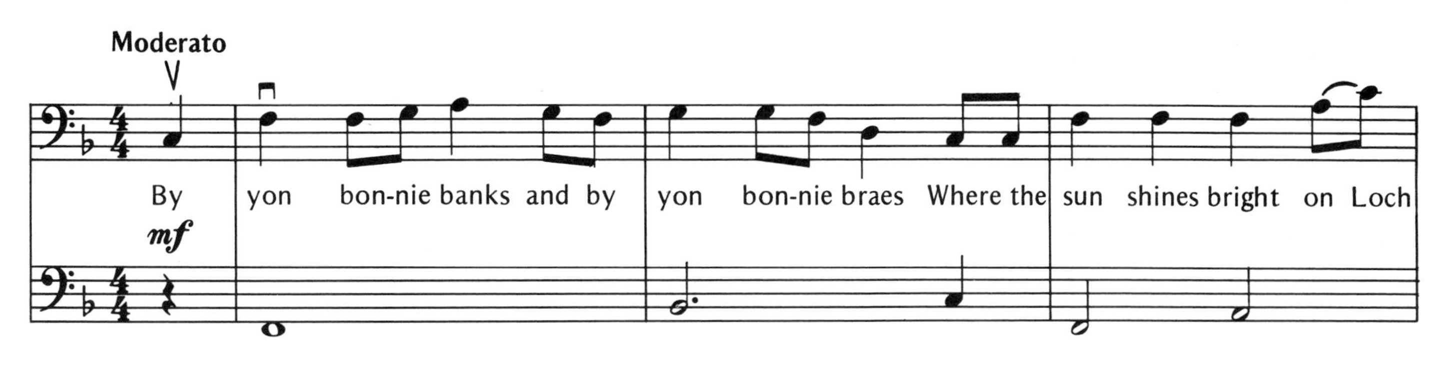
Moderato
By yon bon-nie banks and by yon bon-nie braes Where the sun shines bright on Loch
mf

2 X 1
Lo - mond, Where me and my true love were e - ver wont to be, On the

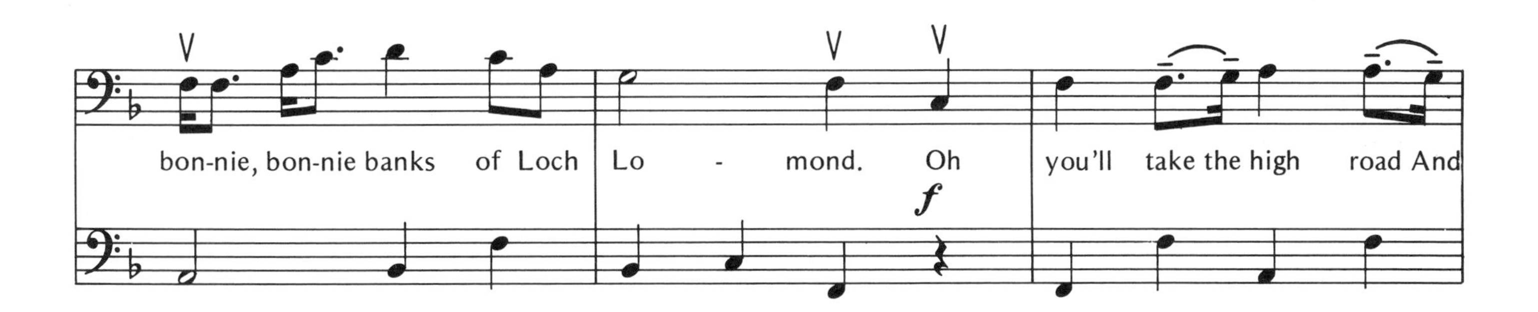
bon-nie, bon-nie banks of Loch Lo - mond. Oh you'll take the high road And
f

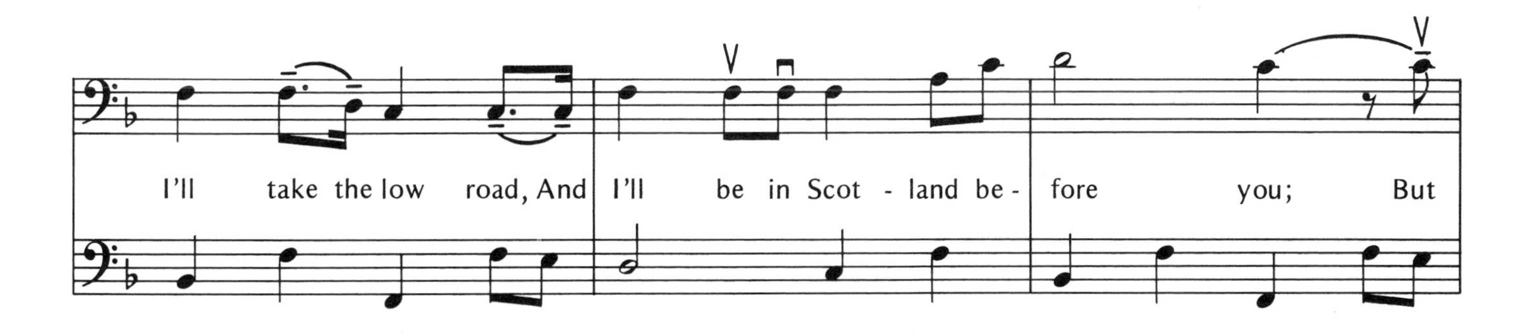
I'll take the low road, And I'll be in Scot - land be - fore you; But

2 X 1
me and my true love will ne-ver meet a-gain, On the bon-nie, bon-nie banks of Loch Lo - mond.
mf

98 Concerto theme

Stamitz

99 Waltz

Weber

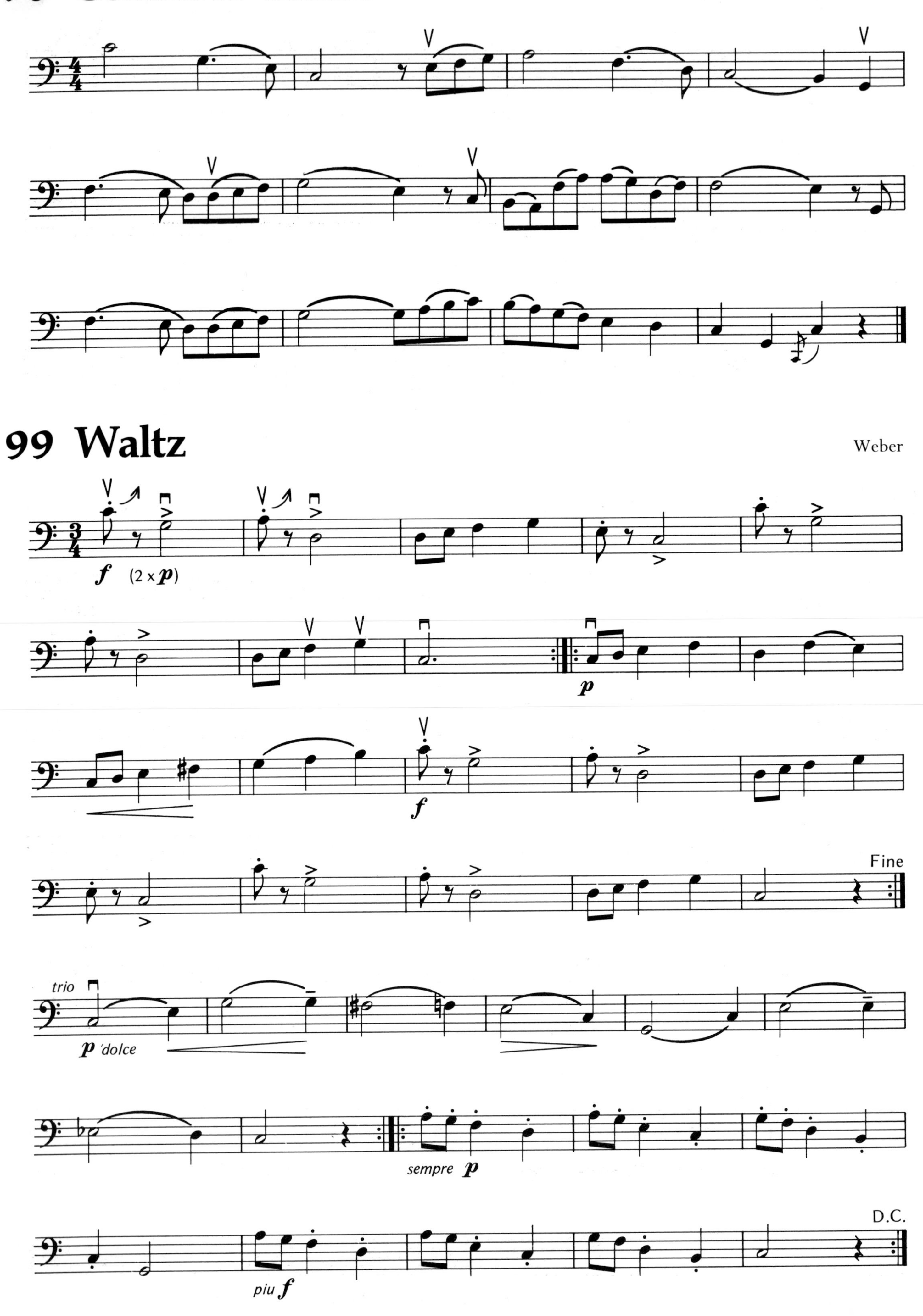

f
(2 x p)
p
f
Fine
trio
p dolce
sempre p
D.C.
piu f

100 Sailing

Gavin Sutherland

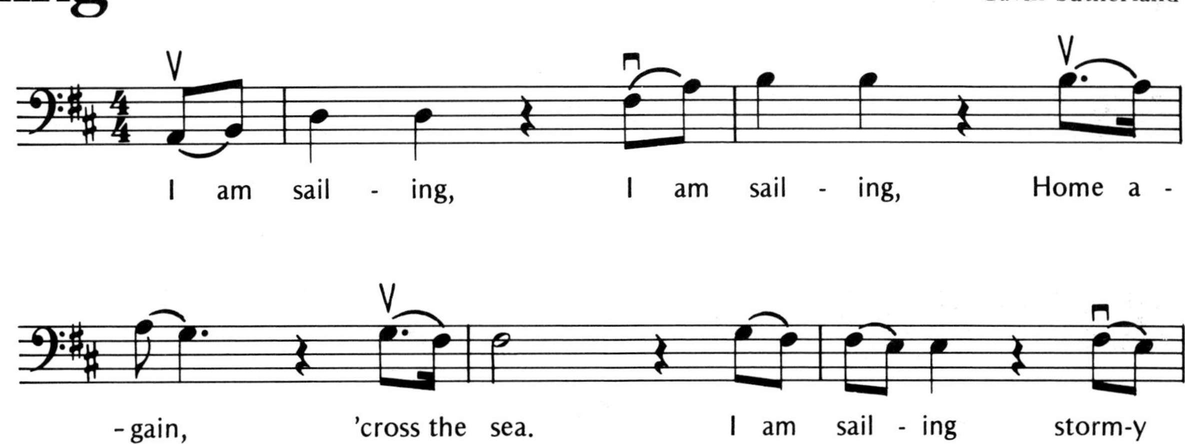
I am sail - ing, I am sail - ing, Home a -
- gain, 'cross the sea. I am sail - ing storm-y

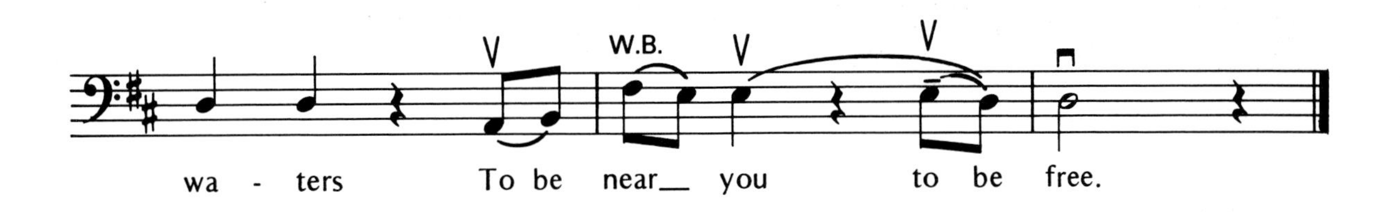
W.B.
wa - ters To be near__ you to be free.

101 Home on the range

North American

Oh, give me a home where the buf - fa - lo roam, Where the
deer and the an - te - lope play; Where sel - dom is
heard a dis - cou - rag - ing word, And the skies are not cloud - y all
day. Home, home on the range, Where the
deer and the an - te - lope play; Where sel - dom is heard a dis -
cou - rag - ing word, And the skies are not cloud-y all day.

102 Over the earth

words: Ruth Brown
music: Scottish adpd and arr Herbert Wiseman, 1886–1966

Andante
mf
O - ver the earth is a mat of green, O - ver the green is dew,
O - ver the dew are the arch - ing trees,
O - ver the trees the blue.
f
A - cross the blue are scud - ding clouds,
O - ver the clouds, the sun,
mf
O - ver it all is the love of God,
Bless - ing us ev - 'ry - one.
p morendo
Bless - ing us ev - 'ry - one.

103 Swing low, sweet chariot

spiritual

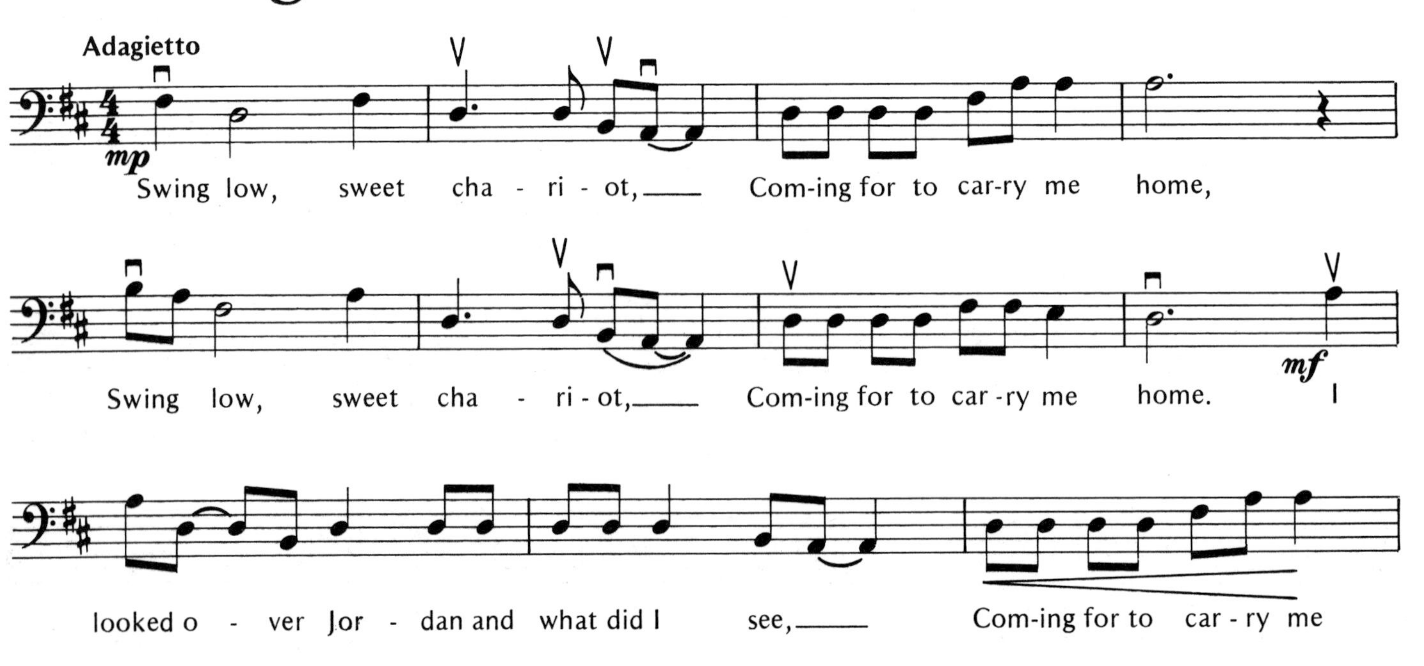
Adagietto
mp
Swing low, sweet cha - ri - ot, Com-ing for to car-ry me home,
Swing low, sweet cha - ri - ot, Com-ing for to car - ry me home.
mf
I looked o - ver Jor - dan and what did I see, Com-ing for to car - ry me

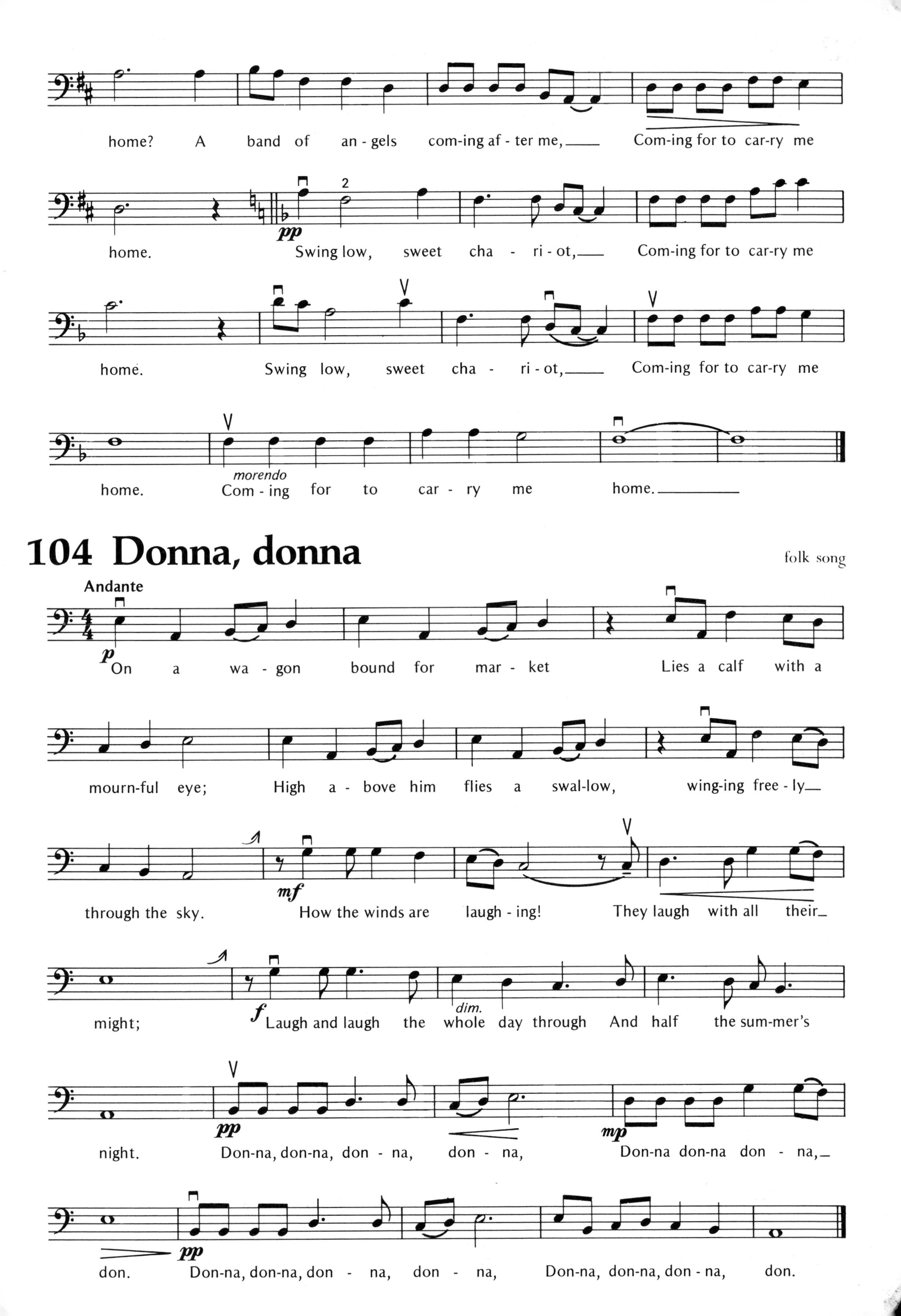
home? A band of an - gels com-ing af - ter me, Com-ing for to car-ry me
home. Swing low, sweet cha - ri - ot, Com-ing for to car-ry me
pp
home. Swing low, sweet cha - ri - ot, Com-ing for to car-ry me
home. Com - ing for to car - ry me home.
morendo
104 Donna, donna
folk song
Andante
p On a wa - gon bound for mar - ket Lies a calf with a
mourn-ful eye; High a - bove him flies a swal-low, wing-ing free - ly
through the sky. How the winds are laugh - ing! They laugh with all their
mf
might; Laugh and laugh the whole day through And half the sum-mer's
f
dim.
night. Don-na, don-na, don - na, don - na, Don-na don-na don - na,
pp
mp
don. Don-na, don-na, don - na, don - na, Don-na, don-na, don - na, don.
pp

105 Old French song

Tchaikovsky

p
p
mp
mf
p
rit.

106 Greensleeves

English

Andantino
mp
mf
dim.
mp
mf
dim.
mp

107 The entertainer

Scott Joplin

I — I A line between repeated fingering means slide the finger up or down.

108 The swan

Saint-Saëns

Andantino Grazioso
p
2 X 4 1 3
2 2 4
4 X 1 1 2 4 1X2 4 X 1
4
2 X 4
W.B.
point
2 X 4 1 3
W.B.
point
mf
rit.
lento
dim.
pp

109 The ash-grove

English words: John Oxenford
music: traditional Welsh

Andantino
mf espress.
The ash - grove how grace - ful, how plain - ly 'tis speak-ing, The

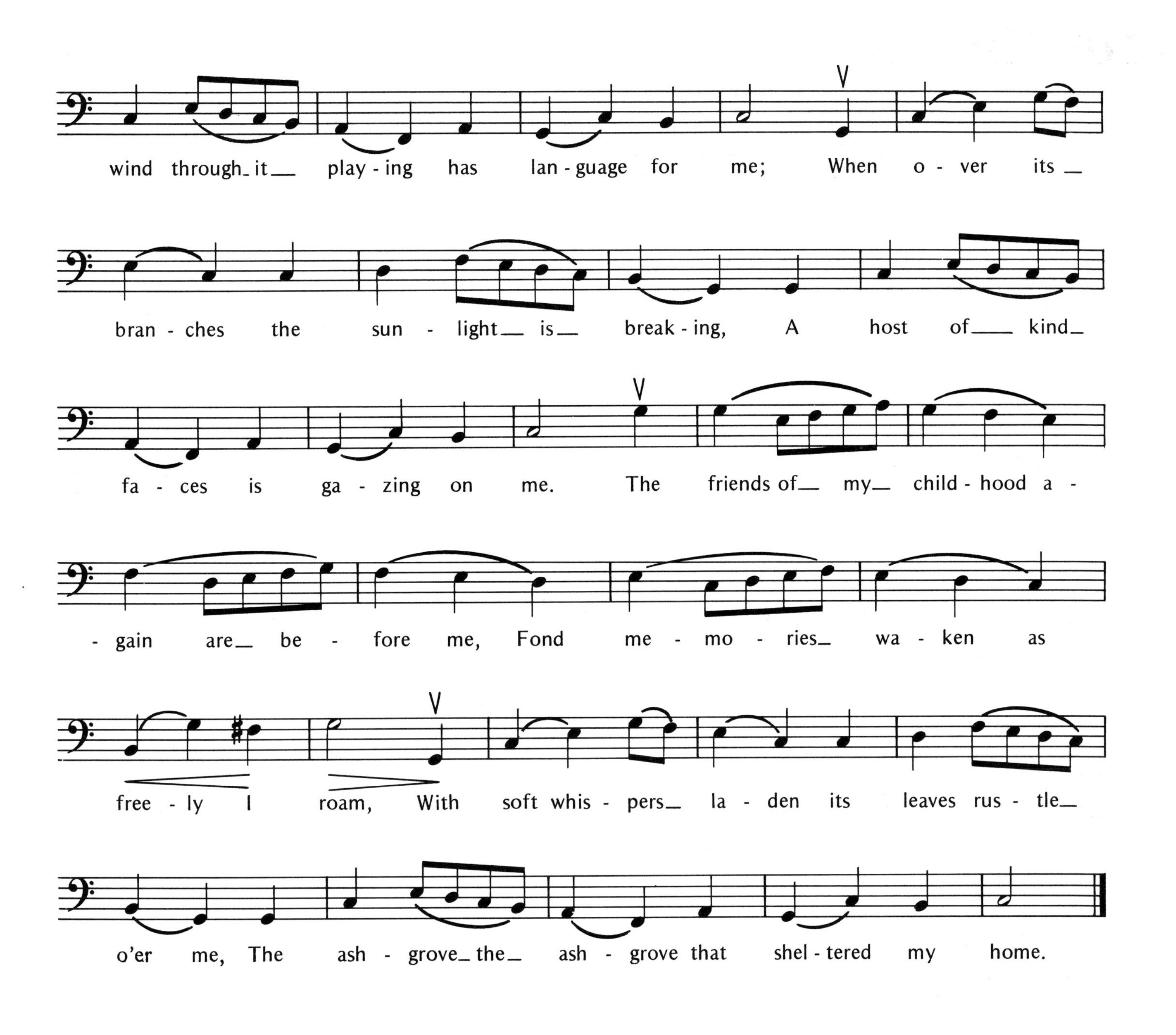
wind through_ it__ play - ing has lan - guage for me; When o - ver its __
bran - ches the sun - light__ is__ break - ing, A host of___ kind_
fa - ces is ga - zing on me. The friends of__ my__ child - hood a -
- gain are__ be - fore me, Fond me - mo - ries__ wa - ken as
free - ly I roam, With soft whis - pers__ la - den its leaves rus - tle__
o'er me, The ash - grove_ the_ ash - grove that shel - tered my home.

110 Theme from the cello concerto

Dvořák

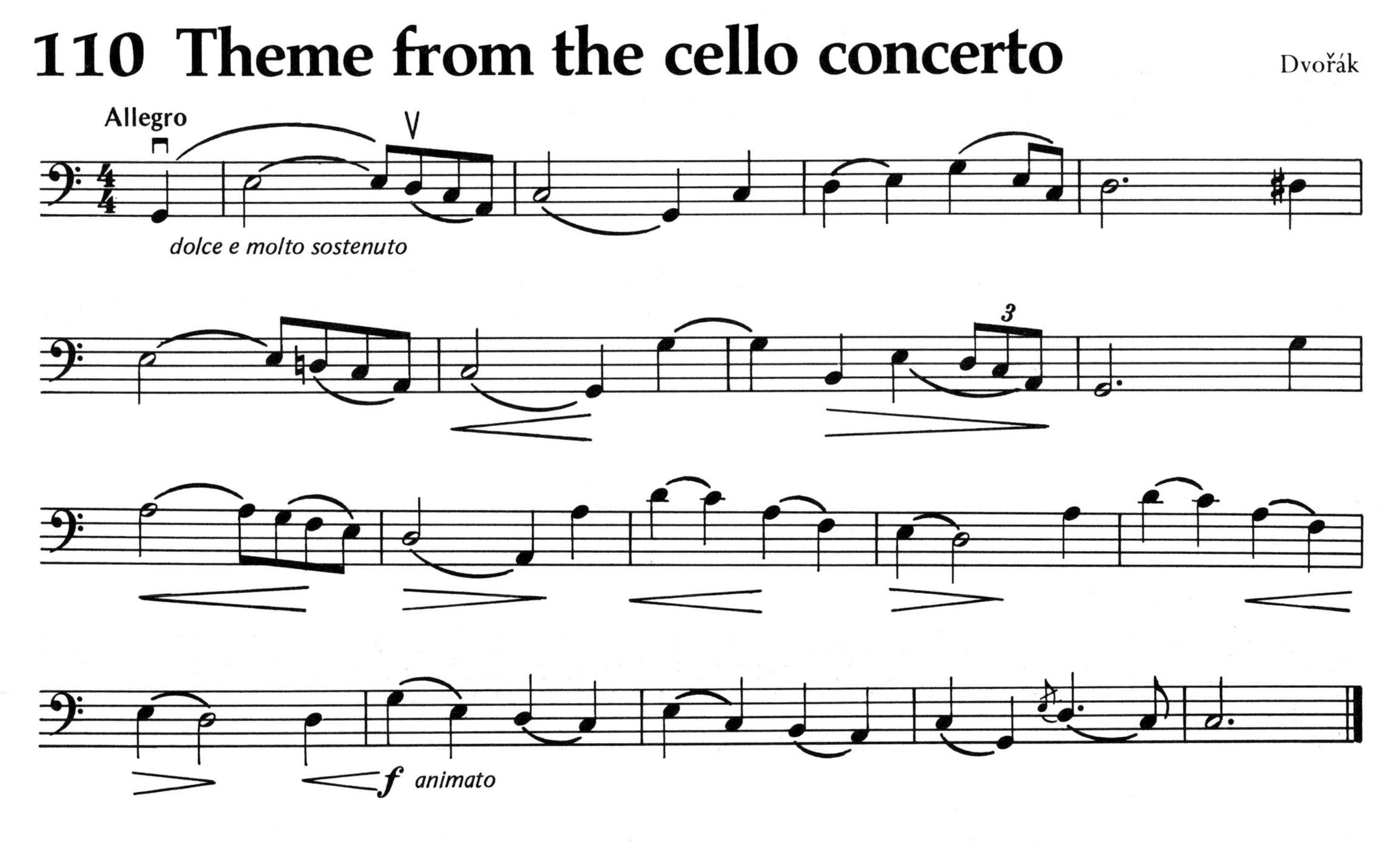
Allegro
dolce e molto sostenuto
3
f animato

Scales and arpeggios

All the scales and arpeggios can be played with slurred or separate bows.

C major (separate bows)
W.B.
point
W.B.
heel
W.B.
W.B.
arpeggio
D major (slurred bows)
1 X 2
1 X 2
1 3
1 3
1X 4
0 3
F major
4
2
G major
3
A major
1 X 2
1 X 2
1 X 4
B flat major
2 4 X
1X 2
X 1
2 X 1
2
D major
3
3
C minor: melodic
2
1 3
2 X 1
2
harmonic
2
1 X 3
3 X 1
2
arpeggio

G minor: melodic
harmonic
arpeggio
D minor: melodic
harmonic
arpeggio
Dominant sevenths:
C major
G major
F major
Rhythmic variations: practise with all scales.
etc
play at point, heel
and middle of bow
point
heel
or
etc

Glossary

⊓	down bow, start at the heel
V	up bow, start at the point
W.B.	use the whole length of the bow
point	stay at the point of the bow
heel	stay at the heel of the bow
↗	lift the bow
X	extension between 1st & 2nd fingers
	zig-zag ⊓ V ⊓ using the whole bow
	zig-zag V ⊓ V using the whole bow
┌──┐	keep fingers on the string

forte, f	loud
piano, p	soft
mezzo forte, mf	quite loud
mezzo piano, mp	quite soft
fortissimo, ff	very loud
pianissimo, pp	very soft

a tempo	back to regular pace
accelerando (accel)	gradually faster
adagietto	slowly, but less slow than adagio
adagio	slowly
allegretto	briskly
allegro	quickly
andante	at leisurely pace
andantino	a little quicker than andante
arco	play with the bow
crescendo (cresc)	gradually louder
D C (da capo)	go back to the beginning
diminuendo (dim)	gradually softer
dolce	sweetly
fine	the end
grazioso	gracefully
largo	very slowly
lento	slowly
meno	less
moderato	at moderate pace
	(allegro moderato = moderately quick)
molto	much, very
piu	more
pizzicato (pizz)	pluck the string
poco	a little
presto	fast
rallentando (rall)	gradually slower
ritardando (rit)	immediately slower
sempre	always
	(sempre pizz = all plucked)

Acknowledgements

The following have kindly granted permission for the reprinting of the copyright material:

Amadeo-Brio Music Corporation for 67 *Morningtown ride*; © Amadeo Music. International copyright secured.

Boosey & Hawkes Music Publishers Ltd for 21 *Canon*; (from Mikrokosmos - Bartok arr Suchoff) © copyright 1940 by Hawkes & Son (London) Ltd. Definitive edition © copyright 1987 by Hawkes & Son (London) Ltd. Reprinted by permission of Bocsey & Hawkes Music Publishers Ltd. And for 49 *An Eriskay love-lilt* from 'Songs of the Hebrides' by permission of the Estate of Marjory Kennedy-Fraser © copyright 1909 Boosey & Co Ltd.

Philip Clarke for 40 *Abracadabra staccato* © Philip Clarke.

Peter Davey for 76 *Theme from 'The bridges of Paris'* © 1988 Peter Davey.

De Toorts, Haarlem for 84 *Porcupine's lullaby (Stekelvarkentjes Wiegelied)*; from 'Dikkertje Dap en 18 andere Liedjes' (Paul Chr Van Westering /Annie M G Schmidt) 10th printing 1997.

Noel Gay Music Ltd for 33 *Thank U very much*. Words and music by Michael McGear. © copyright 1967 Noel Gay Music Company Ltd, 8/9 Frith Street, London W1. Used by permission of Music Sales Ltd. All rights reserved. International copyright secured.

Ronnie Hazlehurst Music for 83 *Last of the summer wine* © Ronnie Hazlehurst MS.

David Higham Associates Ltd for the words of 68 *Morning has broken*, by Eleanor Farjeon from 'Enlarged Songs of Praise' © 1931 published by Oxford University Press.

Island Music for 100 *Sailing*. Words and music by Gavin Sutherland. © copyright 1972 by Island Music Ltd, 47 British Grove, London W4. Used by permission of Music Sales Ltd. All rights reserved. International copyright secured.

Kensington Music Ltd for 29 *Last night I had the strangest dream* © 1950 and 1955 Folkways Music Publishing Inc, Assigned to Kensington Music Ltd, London SW10 0SZ. All rights reserved. International copyright secured. Used by permission.

Robert Kingston Music Ltd for 36 *Dance of the cuckoos* (ku ku) by T Marvin Hatley. © copyright 1930, 1932 Hatley Music Company USA. Controlled throughout the Eastern Hemisphere by Robert Kingston (Music) Limited, 43 Fairfield Road, Uxbridge, Middlesex. Used by permission of Music Sales Ltd. All rights reserved. International copyright secured.

Music Sales Ltd for 64 *All my loving*. Words and music by John Lennon & Paul McCartney. © copyright 1963 Northern Songs. Used by permission of Music Sales Ltd. All rights reserved. International copyright secured. And for 82 *Nowhere man*. Words and music by John Lennon & Paul McCartney. © copyright 1965 Northern Songs. Used by permission of Music Sales Ltd. All rights reserved. International copyright secured.

Oxford University Press for the words of 14 *Andrew mine, Jasper mine*, from 'Three Moravian Carols' © 1962, Oxford University Press. Reprinted by permission. And for the music of 102 *Over the earth is a mat of green*, Scots tune adapted and arranged by Herbert Wiseman from 'Children Praising' © 1937 Oxford University Press. Reprinted by permission.

Maja Passchier for 34 *Valse triste* © 1989 Maja Passchier.

Stainer & Bell Ltd for 27 *Lullaby of the spinning wheel, (The virgin's cradle hymn)* words translated by S T Coleridge © 1936 Stainer & Bell Ltd.

Warner Chappell Music Ltd and Cherry Lane Music for 43 *Puff the Magic Dragon*, composed by Peter Yarrow & Leonard Lipton © 1963 Pepamar Music Corp / WB Music Corp, USA / Honalee Melodies / Cherry Lane Publishing. (70% Warner/Chappell Music Ltd, London W6 8BS. Reproduced by permission of IMP Ltd. 30% published for the world by Cherry Lane Music Publishing Co Inc.)

Every effort has been made to trace and acknowledge copyright owners. If any right has been omitted, the publishers offer their apologies and will rectify this in subsequent editions following notification.

Index of titles